CW00507006

BELIEVE ME

(A Katie Winter FBI Suspense Thriller—Book 4)

Molly Black

Molly Black

Bestselling author Molly Black is author of the MAYA GRAY FBI suspense thriller series, comprising nine books (and counting); of the RYLIE WOLF FBI suspense thriller series, comprising six books (and counting); of the TAYLOR SAGE FBI suspense thriller series, comprising three books (and counting); and of the KATIE WINTER FBI suspense thriller series, comprising six books (and counting).

An avid reader and lifelong fan of the mystery and thriller genres, Molly loves to hear from you, so please feel free to visit www.mollyblackauthor.com to learn more and stay in touch.

ISBN: 978-1-0943-9485-5

BOOKS BY MOLLY BLACK

MAYA GRAY MYSTERY SERIES
GIRL ONE: MURDER (Book #1)
GIRL TWO: TAKEN (Book #2)
GIRL THREE: TRAPPED (Book #3)
GIRL FOUR: LURED (Book #4)
GIRL FIVE: BOUND (Book #5)
GIRL SIX: FORSAKEN (Book #6)
GIRL SEVEN: CRAVED (Book #7)
GIRL EIGHT: HUNTED (Book #8)
GIRL NINE: GONE (Book #9)

RYLIE WOLF FBI SUSPENSE THRILLER
FOUND YOU (Book #1)
CAUGHT YOU (Book #2)
SEE YOU (Book #3)
WANT YOU (Book #4)
TAKE YOU (Book #5)
DARE YOU (Book #6)

TAYLOR SAGE FBI SUSPENSE THRILLER
DON'T LOOK (Book #1)
DON'T BREATHE (Book #2)
DON'T RUN (Book #3)

KATIE WINTER FBI SUSPENSE THRILLER
SAVE ME (Book #1)
REACH ME (Book #2)
HIDE ME (Book #3)
BELIEVE ME (Book #4)
HELP ME (Book #5)
FORGET ME (Book #6)

PROLOGUE

Steve Fury raised his gaze from the snow-covered track ahead of him, to stare at the mountains on the skyline.

Their jagged, icy peaks looked harsh and cruel. This area, far north of Denver, Colorado, was as freezing as it was unforgiving.

He shivered in the icy cold, taking in the emptiness of the landscape surrounding him. It felt all the lonelier since this was the first time he was hiking solo. Usually, he went with his business partner, but things had been strained between them for the past while.

They co-owned an online store that sold outdoor sports gear, and were always looking to test out their own products. Today, he was trying a new pair of hiking boots that promised comfort, fit, and grip in freezing weather. That was certainly the case today. Temperatures had plummeted, and a heavy snowfall last night had obscured parts of the track completely.

He could barely see the way ahead, and right now, he acknowledged sadly that this situation applied to his working life as well.

His shop was struggling. Trade was always low this time of year, and he had to respond to a deluge of 'special offers' from competitors.

He was further hampered by the fact that his partner had already been exploring ways to cash in on their venture. The way things were going, he might well end up the only one working at their business soon, he reflected grimly. He and his business partner were watching each other like two stags at a watering hole. They'd been best friends since they were kids, but now they were talking about taking each other to the cleaners.

He shook his head, and started picking his way over the icy rocks.

If Steve hadn't been reasonably familiar with the route, he would probably not have gone ahead so far, he acknowledged. He really was feeling his way, using the landmarks, going by instinct and memory, out here in the increasingly remote wilderness.

Glancing up at the snow-covered peaks again, he shivered in the chill wind. It was time to head back for the day, he decided, and return to the battlefield that was his business life these days.

1

He didn't even have his cell phone with him. It was in his pack, and that was in the car. He wasn't sure the cell signal could reach out here, in these desolate hills. So he'd have to go somewhere warm, find a signal, and catch up on the calls and emails and orders.

If he remembered correctly, the track made a left turn just past the trees. Once he was clear of them, it looped back toward the local town where he'd parked his car.

He could see the forested, sheltered area ahead. He headed for it, trudging over the snow.

And then, out of nowhere, the track disappeared from under him.

He didn't slip; he didn't fall. It felt as if he just stepped forward into nothingness. Like stepping into an open elevator shaft. The ground ahead of him just wasn't there.

He gasped in shock as the track vanished from under his boots. He was falling, in a sort of slow motion nightmare.

The snowy white world flashed past him, his flailing arms seeking purchase, but slipping off the icy rocks.

And then he hit the ground.

As he did so, he felt a bolt of pain shoot through his thigh.

He groaned, unable to move. In this deep crevasse, something was pinning him painfully. Staring down, his eyes widened in horror as he saw he was skewered by a length of rusty steel rebar. It was firmly embedded in the ground, and he had fallen directly onto it.

The sharpened tip had stabbed all the way through his thigh.

He was pinned to the ground. He couldn't move; he couldn't get out.

He cried out in panic as he saw the rapid, crimson spread of blood over the rocky ground.

His mind was spinning in confusion. He still had no idea how this could have happened. How had the trail just disappeared, channeling him into this steep ravine that had been somehow hidden from view?

But there was no time to piece together the impossible. He was bleeding to death. Without a doubt, this horrific wound would be fatal.

Already, he was starting to feel weak, his head spinning as he fumbled uselessly in his pocket for his phone, averting his eyes from the terrible sight of his leg.

He'd left it in the car, he realized. Shock had obliterated that memory and he'd wasted valuable seconds looking for a phone that wasn't there. All he could do now was call for help and hope that, somehow, someone might hear.

"Help!" he yelled, hearing the tremble in his own voice, feeling cold with fear at how suddenly this routine hike had turned deadly.

He knew shouting was most likely a waste of time. He hadn't seen another hiker since he'd started out. It was too cold, too snowy. People who weren't running from their problems, like him, had stayed indoors.

His vision was starting to blur, he realized, with a surge of fright.

He stared up the rocky precipice to the place where the snow met the sky, wondering if it would be the last thing he saw.

And then, he saw someone looking down.

Hope surged inside him. Somehow, someone had heard.

A big, bulky man was peering over the edge, his large, thick body cutting the skyline and darkening the view. He was wrapped in furs. A hunter, for sure.

"Help me! I've fallen onto a spike! I need a medevac out of here urgently!"

He waited for the guy to call back to him, hoping to hell this man had a phone and that there was signal here.

But the man did nothing. There was no sign of understanding. He just looked down at Steve with a blank expression on his face.

"I need an ambulance!" Steve yelled, gasping in pain. "Help me!" he repeated, his voice cracking with terror and shock as he tried to shout louder. "Please! Medical emergency! Help!"

The big man didn't respond. He just kept looking down.

With a chill, Steve realized he wasn't going to help. He was simply going to watch.

"Why?" he wanted to ask.

He tried to ask the agonized question, but he no longer had the strength. He felt so cold, so numb, he was barely aware of the pain in his leg anymore. The world was fading out, becoming hazy and gray.

The last thing he saw was the big man's face. It had a big, bushy beard, and large, dark eyes as cold as the snow.

The last thing he heard was the sound of his voice. It was deep and hollow, like a cave.

Steve tried to understand what he was saying, but his mind was too far gone.

The frozen world was drifting away from him like a mist. The pain was ebbing from his body.

He heard the big man's voice echo inside his head, over and over. The words didn't make sense, and then they faded away completely as darkness rushed in.

CHAPTER ONE

Katie Winter put her hand on the wooden kitchen door of her old family home, and pushed it open.

Her heart was hammering. She felt more nervous than she did at the start of a criminal takedown. Despite ten years' experience as an FBI agent, this was undoubtedly the scariest moment of her life.

This was the back door of her parents' home, close to Wilson, in the wilderness of northern New York.

She had grown up in this log house bordering Lake Ontario, with her twin sister Josie. They'd been identical tomboys, with their mischievous green eyes and shiny, brown hair that each had worn in a long bob. It had been a wild, adventurous childhood - until it had ended in disaster that had broken her family apart.

At the age of sixteen, a kayaking dare out on the wild, flooding river had turned into disaster when her twin's canoe had capsized and she'd disappeared.

Katie's life had fallen apart. Her relationship with her parents had crumbled.

They'd blamed her for her sister's death.

She'd left home soon afterward and forged her own way in the world. Their estrangement had hurt and confused her so much that she'd thrown herself into her studies, graduating with honors and then joining the FBI to become a specialist in chasing down serial killers.

She'd buried her feelings, her heartbreak, her confusion, in the life of a dedicated law enforcement officer. And she'd become one of the Bureau's most successful agents, fighting crime and putting behind bars some of the most dangerous people in the country.

But she'd always had to live with the pain of rejection. The feeling of blame. She'd always resolved that one day she would come back, and she would try to make things right with them.

They hadn't answered her knock. But she was going inside anyway. A glance through the window had confirmed she would find them in the lounge, where the fire burned and the television blared. There, her parents were hiding away - from her, from each other, and from the world.

Was she brave enough? Was it too late?

Taking a deep breath, she opened the door and walked inside.

"Mom? Dad?"

Her voice sounded tight and scared.

She walked through the kitchen and into the lounge and she saw their astonished gazes swivel to her.

Her father was sitting in an armchair, facing the television. He looked so different from how she remembered. Once rugged and strong, he now looked grayer and more stooped, as if time and tragedy had worn him away.

Katie had inherited her mother's slim build, but her mother was now so thin she looked gaunt. Her brown hair was streaked with gray. The perennial smile that Katie remembered so well from her childhood, had vanished from her face after Josie's disappearance. Now, she looked as if she hadn't smiled since.

Her father was the first to react. He struggled up from the chair.

"What are you doing here? It's been – it's been so many years."

He sounded utterly shocked. His tone was not friendly, but it didn't sound hostile either. It was as if he couldn't decide how he felt about Katie, even though so much time had passed. She thought her father's surprise at seeing her had jolted him right out of any sensible reply.

"Nearly fourteen years, yes," she said. Her mouth felt dry.

"Why?" he asked the single word. She thought his voice was shaking too, now.

"I came back...," her words were trembling on her lips. "I came here to try to make things right."

She glanced at the empty chair where Josie had always sat. It was directly opposite her father, its threadbare cushion faded. It was a painful reminder of all they'd lost.

Her mother was staring at her, speechless, her pale face drained of color and expression.

"Mom? Are you okay?"

She thought she saw the glimmer of tears in her mother's eyes as she gave a small nod, but she couldn't be sure.

Her father was frowning, as if still processing his emotions on seeing her again.

"I don't know what to say to you," he said. "I don't know how to start this conversation."

He sounded as if he wasn't sure he wanted to.

Katie swallowed, feeling a rush of panic.

"I know," she said. "I feel the same. I know this is not a good time. Perhaps there is never going to be a good time, but I just wanted a chance to talk to you. I've wanted this for ages."

She found it hard to breathe. She couldn't think straight. Her hands felt icy cold.

"I've missed you, Dad."

"We missed you too, Katie," he said. "Please, sit."

He sat again, his face pale. She didn't even glance at Josie's chair, but perched on the wooden dining room chair in the corner of the room.

"I guess it's time. We need to talk," her mother acknowledged.

But silence followed. It seemed as if none of them knew how to start, to break down the massive barriers she still sensed lay between them. Katie decided to push forward with some general conversation to ease the tension. Not her strong suit, and not what she wanted to say, but at least it was a start.

"How have you been? Are you well?" she asked. "Is the business still going okay?" Her father ran a small boat hire company.

"We're getting by," her father said. "We've downscaled some, but still busy."

"We're good," her mother said. "It's good to see you, Katie. I've felt so bad about this. I have always wondered –"

Her mother stopped herself and shook her head, as if she didn't dare to spill out the rest of that confession.

Her father nodded, clearly understanding what she'd meant to say.

Katie felt tears prick her eyes. She had expected her return to make her feel emotional, but had thought she'd be able to control herself better. She didn't want to cry in front of them.

"There's something I need to say to you." Katie took a step closer, looking at the floor, speaking the words that had haunted her for years. "I'm so sorry, Mom, Dad," she said. "I'm so sorry that I didn't save Josie. I'm so sorry that she's gone."

She paused, looking up and meeting her mother's eyes.

"I need to say this. I know you blamed me for her death. All these years I've felt that I let you down. I let her down. I hated myself for that."

She felt the atmosphere in the room darkening. They didn't want to talk about this. But it had to be done! There was simply no way of ignoring the subject. Her twin's presence had never felt as immediate as it did during this moment.

"I don't want to speak about this," her mother muttered. "I can't."

Her dad's face now looked hard and closed.

"I know this is tough," Katie implored. "But we have to talk about it. I - I want to know what happened. What you found out. I need closure on this, because I never knew the full story."

"It's not the right time for that!" Now she heard anger in her father's voice.

"Clearly," she said. "But when, then? When do you want to speak about this? Because we can't not speak about it. We need to get this out in the open!"

She was inwardly berating herself for having approached this too quickly. She'd wanted to push through the pain, but had ended up being too forceful, and destroying the tenuous balance that she'd briefly achieved with her estranged parents. She should have worked up to it more slowly and been more subtle.

But how? How could you approach such a topic in a subtle way?

"We can't discuss that!" her mother flashed back.

"Why not?" Katie asked, deciding she was committed to her path. "Why can't we talk about it now? Avoiding it is not making it go away, and it's killing us inside. All of us! What happened after Josie disappeared has been the most painful part of my life. I need to get closure, so that I can move on. And so that you can!"

She took a deep breath. It was time to say what she knew.

"I was in Northfields prison recently," she said, and saw their faces change, horror and expectation in their eyes.

"I saw Charles Everton. I spoke to him. I asked him about Josie. But he said she was the one who begged him to save her. The one he never killed. Do you know about that? What does it mean?"

She stared at them pleadingly, but realized it was too late.

She'd lost her chance. The anger in her father's face told her that even before he spoke.

"Get out!" he said.

"What?"

"You heard me. Get out of my house. If this is what you came for, you're not welcome here."

"Dad, listen!"

"I said, get out! You've caused enough hurt. Leave, now."

Katie stood gazing at her father helplessly, trying to find the words to calm him down. Before she could, he was on his feet again, glaring at her.

"Leave!" he repeated.

And then her mother's words cut her like a knife. She was staring at Katie, with mingled fury and pain in her eyes.

"How dare you come here and open up all these wounds!"

She was shaking with anguish, Katie saw.

"It's not like we don't have enough to deal with. And now you want to bring it all up again. I can't accept this! I never want to think about it."

All Katie could do was gape at her, stunned by the vehemence of her words.

"Mom –" she murmured.

"Please, Katie. Please go. It's too much. I can't take anymore."

A tear spilled down Katie's cheek. She wiped it away, angry at her weakness. She didn't want to let them see her cry. Not now.

Forcing the tears away, she stood up, turned, and walked out the door. But as she stepped outside, she turned and looked back.

In the midst of her shock, her mind had come up with an unexpected question. Why were they behaving this way? Why were they so vociferously attacking her for these questions? Why were they basically throwing her out of the house?

With a twist of her stomach, Katie wondered if there really was something she didn't yet know about Josie's disappearance. Something they didn't want her to know.

"I'm not letting this go," she insisted. "I will find out what happened. You're proving to me that something did. And when I've found out, I'm going to come back and we're going to talk about it. So please, be ready for it."

She turned away and headed to her car. Her eyes were streaming with tears now, but a fierce resolve burned inside her. Whatever it took, she was going to pursue this. She was going to discover the truth, in the hope it might free her, and her parents, from their pain. And she knew exactly where she was going to start.

CHAPTER TWO

The woman sitting opposite Leblanc in the small Paris bistro reached out and grasped his hand, her dark eyes sparkling. "You should come back here. Permanently, I mean. Not just for the weekend."

Leblanc looked into her eyes and nodded.

"It's something to think about," he agreed, with a smile.

The woman, Eloise Fournier, was slim, elegant, and attractive. She was an old friend of Leblanc's that he had first met in Paris years ago, when she had been a prison warden.

Now, on re-acquaintance, and after two glasses of cabernet sauvignon, he realized that there was more to the friendship, and that a romantic spark had the potential to flame.

It was as if her words opened up a different set of choices to Leblanc. He could visualize a possible future for himself, returned to Paris. He could resume his career as a detective in the French police. And if he came back, then for sure, this spark could go further.

It was a nice dream. But there were complications. Too many to list.

For a start, Eloise was not just a pretty face, but a tough woman in a hard job. She was now in charge of security at the Paris maximum-security prison where Leblanc's investigation partner, Cecile Roux, had been murdered and where the killer, Hugo Gagnon, was now incarcerated. Eloise had been promoted into the new position soon after the riots. That was when Leblanc, shocked, grief-stricken and bereaved, had gotten to know her a little better.

He felt conflicted now, because he knew that Eloise could make sure Gagnon had a hard time inside. Security had many powers within a prison environment. Eloise could ensure that that Gagnon never got privileges, was always disciplined to the maximum for any infractions, was never allowed any contraband. She could make sure that he suffered as he was meant to during his life sentence.

Leblanc knew it would be unethical to ask her for this favor, and that he shouldn't even be thinking this way. But disturbingly, he found that in his mind, he imagined more.

He imagined this unpleasant, violent man being confined to solitary for months. Word was they all hated him inside. He already slept in a cell on his own, for this reason.

In his deepest, darkest dreams, Leblanc imagined a tipping point occurring, a moment where a situation was allowed to flare. In his most private dreams of revenge, he imagined this man being killed in prison violence just the way he had taken Cecile's life.

He wanted Gagnon dead. In the moments of pain that he still endured, Leblanc imagined looking into the killer's eyes as his life slowly ebbed away, staring down at his dead body and knowing he had finally paid the ultimate price for what he'd done.

Leblanc knew this could only ever be a fantasy, and one which made him feel at once guilty and vindicated. Reality didn't work that way, and particularly not with Eloise in charge of security.

It was just dreams. He was taking refuge in dreams, to avoid having to deal with the fallout from a tragedy he still hadn't fully processed.

Eloise sensed his conflict. She squeezed his hand.

"What is it?" she asked, but Leblanc didn't answer.

He squeezed her hand back. Their eyes locked.

"I don't know if I am ready to come back," Leblanc admitted, forcing his thoughts to return to her question and not his own tormented thoughts.

"You've been away two years. We miss you. You have a lot of ties here. A lot of friends."

He nodded. That was why he was back. Yesterday, he'd met Cecile's family at her grave, to commemorate what would have been her thirtieth birthday. It had been a solemn occasion. Her family was still distraught, and their obvious grief had made Leblanc feel guilty all over again that he hadn't been there to help her when she was killed.

It was a flying visit, for the weekend only. Today was Sunday, and he was catching up with Eloise before getting on a plane for home later that evening.

Home. The word surprised him, but it was true that he had started thinking of his apartment in Sault Ste Marie, on the border of Canada and the USA, as his home now.

He perceived his role in the special cross-border task force as his new life and career.

And he was growing closer to his new investigation partner, Katie Winter. He valued what they had, but at the same time, the closeness brought with it a sense of fear, because Leblanc knew all too well that the worst could happen when investigating dangerous crimes.

"How are things going there on the US-Canada border?" Eloise asked.

"Good," Leblanc said, with a smile. "The team's growing closer. We're working well together. It's been an adjustment, but we're getting there. And we've had some interesting cases."

"In the icy cold!" Eloise reminded him teasingly. "Never your favorite, if I remember."

"I have to admit, working there has made me think about the things I miss here. Spring in Paris being one."

Eloise smiled. "Give more thought to coming back here. Paris is your home. You've been away long enough."

Leblanc smiled back, but inside, he felt thoroughly conflicted.

What were his real motives for considering coming back to Paris?

It felt brutal to force himself to confront the truth.

Paris was his home, it was familiar, he knew and loved the city and had loved his job.

But would he return with good intentions to start afresh after a break? Or would he be running away from what he had now, in Sault Ste Marie?

That raised a tough question he had been trying to avoid thinking about.

What have I become?

He had been a decent detective. He'd been a good police officer. But, in many ways, he was not the same person he had been two years ago. The loss of Cecile had changed him. He had become someone he didn't like or desire to be. Harder, colder. Moodier for sure, and with more thoughts of personal revenge taking root in his mind.

Now, he was being forced to face himself, and he didn't like what he saw.

He knew it was natural to want to punish his killer. But Gagnon was already being punished with a life sentence in jail. And any thoughts of further retribution surely meant that Leblanc was no better than that thug. He had no right to ask Eloise to treat Gagnon any differently, or punish him any worse, than his fellow inmates.

A shiver went down his spine.

Perhaps that was another reason it was better to stay away. Because he didn't want the lines to become blurred. If he was tempted to pursue revenge, he might find that he had become someone he could never forgive.

But yet, he couldn't help thinking that maybe staying away was cowardice, too, because he was avoiding the pain, rather than working through it.

"I'm not sure," he said, looking at Eloise. "I've been considering it a lot lately."

"I know it won't be easy to come back to work here. But you will have so many opportunities if you do."

"I can't make a decision right now," Leblanc said. "I have committed to this task force, at least for the winter months. When summer comes, perhaps I can reconsider."

"Until then, you had better stay in touch," she encouraged him.

"I promise I will."

That, at least, was a promise he could keep.

"What time is your flight?" she asked.

"Six-thirty," Leblanc said. "I have to go and pack now. I'm sorry."

Eloise smiled. "No need to apologize," she said. "I know you have to go."

They both stood up.

They hugged warmly. He gave her a quick kiss on the cheek and then they parted. As he walked away, he glanced back, and saw her looking after him.

"This isn't goodbye," Leblanc called to her. "I'll speak to you soon."

Her face lit up as she smiled.

"I look forward to it," she said.

He strode away, not wanting to acknowledge or confront the conflict that surged in his mind when he thought of Eloise and his old colleagues in Paris, and Katie and the task team on the border. He had big decisions ahead.

Leblanc hoped that in the next few days, he would be able to think more clearly about where he would commit to working, and who he would allow himself to love.

CHAPTER THREE

FBI Special Agent Martins felt adrenaline spike inside him as the wooden shack came into view. Reaching it had been a long, tough slog through the Colorado snow.

"We're here," he radioed to headquarters.

"Is it in the right location?" the control room radioed back.

"Identical coordinates," he confirmed.

The tip-off earlier that day had led them on this cold, dangerous chase-down, following the tracks of the killer who had been terrorizing the area.

In recent weeks, he'd caused four bloody, painful, and terrifying deaths by setting physical traps along the seldom-used hiking routes.

The first one, the police had thought must have been intended for an animal but claimed a human by mistake. Even so, they had launched an urgent investigation to see who the irresponsible idiot was setting traps like that, which were totally illegal in construction and located along paths that humans frequented.

Before they had gotten far with the investigation, two more deaths had followed in quick succession. Witness reports had been gathered, and from the accounts of those who'd seen him, the police realized that someone in the area was deliberately setting these traps to catch hikers or passersby.

At that stage, the FBI had been called in, and they'd been working around the clock to catch this psycho. They had scoured the area, questioned hundreds of locals, offered a reward, and followed up on every tip they received.

Yesterday he'd killed again, and this was the first time that they had received evidence leading to his location, as he'd fled from the site of the crime. They'd had a lucky break, thanks to an eyewitness who had followed him.

That had led them to this shack, cradled among craggy mountains in inhospitable terrain in the wilderness, about a hundred miles northwest of Denver. They had confirmed for sure that this was his bolt hole, and where they expected to find him now.

As Martins forged closer through the snow, what he saw in front of him was stark and shocking. As a seasoned agent who had worked on the front lines for years, and taken down numerous criminals, he felt shivers cascade down his spine.

The place was surrounded by skulls on poles. The bones, stark and pale, looked yellow against the whiteness of the snow.

This crude wooden cabin didn't look like a home. It looked like a weird fortress. Or a tomb.

He saw a few smaller animal skulls. Those must be foxes. But there were larger ones, too. That one looked like a cougar, that one like a bear.

He caught his breath as he saw an unmistakably human skull at the center of the display, speared on a wooden stake. Behind him, he heard his team gasp, and murmur among themselves, as they too realized what was there.

The sight of those dark, staring eye-sockets chilled him in a visceral way.

What did this mean? Was this the lair of a psychopath? A madman? Martins shook his head, trying to rid his mind of the disturbing thoughts.

"Okay, people," he said. "We need to be careful."

Glancing around, he saw the three other agents looked as spooked as he did.

But this was their job, and they had to do it.

"We move in," Martins said. "Keep low. Remember, the suspect could be inside. He's probably armed and he is most definitely dangerous."

Martins guessed the psycho they were chasing would be a formidable opponent. He was cunning and agile; he was savage and skilled.

They didn't yet know his name, but one of the witnesses from the general store nearby, who'd given them information, had thought he was called Wolfe. Martins suspected that was a pseudonym. Apart from that, they knew he was tall, strong, and 'shaggy looking' as the witnesses had described.

As he made his way closer to the cabin, he hoped that the suspect was inside and that they'd surprise him. They needed to corner this guy, to capture him, arrest him, and lock him away. They needed to end this, once and for all.

They had to. They could not risk him getting away or escaping.

He shivered as he thought of this disastrous outcome. A man like this would not be easy to recapture.

He carefully and quietly made his way up the front steps of the cabin. He looked around. The tiny window near the doorway was dark, and he could see no movement inside.

"FBI!" he yelled, hammering on the door. "You are under arrest! Wolfe, come out, immediately, with your hands in the air!"

He waited, feeling his heart pound, all his senses alert.

There was no sound from within.

It was time, now. He had to show courage and leadership, and storm the door.

But, at that moment, his radio crackled again.

"Martins?" the control room questioned.

"We're about to enter the premises," he snapped back. "No sign of the suspect, though."

"We have updated information and a probable sighting."

He paused. "Where?"

Control wouldn't have contacted him now without good reason. Even at this critical point in the takedown, he tried to listen calmly.

"He may have fled the state. We've just received the police report. A man fitting his description stole a car a couple of hours ago, at a truck stop on the highway heading north. The owner saw him drive away."

"Okay. There's no sign of him here."

"This hideout may be a dead end."

Martins nodded. That was the way this felt. He'd had experience of raids, and there had been no sight, sound, or even sense of anyone hiding inside. He was disappointed, but not surprised, that Wolfe had instinctively known his time here was up.

"We'll search the premises anyway. Hopefully there'll be some evidence, or something linking him to his next planned bolt hole."

"Good luck, agent."

The eye-sockets of the skull felt like they were staring into him, as if they were watching him. This place was as spooky as hell, but it was empty. Abandoned.

Martins got off the radio.

"Strong probability this place is empty, and our suspect has fled north," he updated them quietly.

"There's no sign of him here," the agent behind him agreed. "It snowed this morning, and there's no footprints around."

"Let's go in now, search, and gather evidence."

Martins stepped forward, and kicked the door in.

It swung open with a bang, rusty hinges screaming, and he breathed in the musty smell of the gloom beyond.

On the floor there was a crumpled, filthy rug. A window on the back wall had its shutters closed, with only a faint rim of light leaking in.

Even though the suspect had fled, Martins kept his gun at the ready as he entered the cabin. He stopped in the doorway and looked around.

It was cold and dark, full of old junk. There was a mildewed bucket, with a single dirty rag in it. The few pieces of furniture looked as if they had been built by hand. They were scuffed, worn, and badly made.

He moved forward, treading over the rug.

But to his dismay, the rug was not covering solid floor. Even as he realized, trying desperately to jump back, the ground fell away from under him.

He plummeted through the gap and, as he did so, he screamed in agony as he felt the steel teeth of a bear trap snap shut on his leg.

He sprawled forward, hitting his head on the edge of the pit as the trap clanged closed.

Pain consumed him as the steel teeth bit deeply into his thigh. He gasped as he felt blood pumping from the wounds. The weight of the trap was heavy on his leg. He tried to jerk himself free, grasping at the narrow sides of the pit, but he couldn't move.

The trap was like a vise, crushing his limb, cutting deep into his flesh.

"Help me! Help me!" he yelled. This was a disaster. He stared down at the terrible sight, paralyzed by shock and pain. His leg was smashed, torn. From the breathlessness and dizziness he already felt, he realized that the vicious steel teeth had pierced his femoral artery. The pain was excruciating, and he knew he had only a few minutes left to live.

"Can we pull you out of there, boss?" One of the other agents rushed forward.

"No! There's a bear trap here. My leg is pinned!" It was agony to try to move, and the trap felt immovable. It must be somehow secured to the bottom of the pit.

Martin's voice wavered as he realized there was no easy way out of this narrow, deep hole. His leg was pouring blood.

17

"We have to do something! Have to get him out somehow!" The other agents rushed around him, but already, their voices seemed distant and faraway. He knew he was going to bleed out before they could figure a way to get him out of the hole.

Only now did he realize how dangerous, how devious this killer was. He had been the hunter, but he had become the prey.

"Find him," he said weakly. "Just find him. Whatever it takes."

He stared up at the ceiling, feeling his heart flutter and stall as the voices faded away and silence rushed in.

CHAPTER FOUR

Katie Winter stood in a small room inside the Northfields Maximum Security prison, staring expectantly through the thick steel grille that separated her from the secure room opposite.

She'd been inside this prison recently, questioning a suspect while on a case. Knowing that Charles Everton, her sister's suspected killer, was incarcerated here, she'd taken a few minutes to speak to him.

What he'd said had given her more questions than answers. Questions that had burned at her mind and given her sleepless nights.

She'd resolved she was never again going to lose focus while on a case. It was unfair to let her team down. But she wasn't on a case now. It was Monday morning, and she had requested the morning off from her work. She'd asked direct permission to interview this prisoner again, and the authorities had granted it.

Today, Katie was here in her personal capacity. She was going to demand the truth, and clearer answers. She was not going to allow Charles Everton to toy with her this time.

The interview room was bare and cold. It always was. The only thing that mattered was the chair before her, and the man who would soon be sitting in it.

There he was. She drew in a sharp breath as the doors to the secure room beyond opened and Everton walked in, flanked by two correctional officers. They escorted him to the chair and he sat, regarding her with his pale, lifeless eyes. She shivered as she met his cold gaze. He looked unreadable. His face was harsh, his hair flecked with gray. His features were hard.

He was a man who had killed for pleasure, many times, before being locked away. His evil was immense.

Briefly, Katie doubted herself, wondering what hope she had.

She felt intensely nervous, as if this was a make-or-break moment, and her own actions would decide its success or failure.

He looked directly at her, and although there was no hint of guilt in his face, his eyes gleamed with malevolence.

"What do you want?" he asked softly.

"Charles Everton, I want the truth," she said firmly.

"The truth?" His tone was mocking.

"That's why I'm here," she said.

"I hardly think you have a right to ask me questions."

"I deserve answers," she explained, trying to sound reasonable.

"I've told you what I know. Quite recently, in fact. Were you supposed to speak to me that time, I wonder? Did you get into trouble with your partner, for coming to talk to me?" he asked.

He was perceptive. And cruel. Katie forced herself not to react to this accurate jibe.

"You didn't answer me satisfactorily," she said.

"You want to ask more?"

"What happened to my sister?" she asked, feeling her stomach twist. "You saw her that day, near the river? Didn't you? Tell me what happened then."

He looked at her for a moment, and she shivered as she saw his eyes harden.

"I have told you all I know," he insisted.

"If you had, I wouldn't be here, asking you again."

"You think you can force me to talk? How?"

She saw his eyes gleaming, and realized he was taunting her. He was goading her, aiming to torment her, to upset her. His tone was mocking.

Why was he doing that?

Katie thought fast. Over and above the fact that he was a psychopath who reveled in others' misery, she wondered if this conversation was unsettling him. Perhaps he was taunting her because he was trying to pressure her to leave.

"Did you kill her?" she asked, trying to remain calm. She needed to, even though she was screaming inside. If he was uneasy, she had to push this. Perhaps she might then get the truth.

"I don't even remember who your sister is," Everton hedged, smiling slightly.

"Are you trying to hide something? Is it because you know you're guilty and you're afraid? Or because you regret what you did?" Katie persisted. Rage and fear warred inside her, but with an effort, she kept her face expressionless.

"Afraid?" He gave her a mocking smile. "Of what? Facing the truth? Or afraid you're going to leave here with nothing?"

She stared back, wondering what she could say next to break through his defenses.

"Are you afraid of me?" she asked suddenly.

"No. Why should I be?"

"Because I'm here to get the truth out of you. No matter what it takes. You told me she begged you to save her, that she was the one you never killed. What did you mean by that?"

"Well, she did beg, that's a fact," he said, his voice cold.

"She begged? When? What did she say?" Excitement flared inside her at this snippet of information.

"I don't have to answer your questions." He was shutting down. Regretting what he'd said.

"No, you don't. But I'm going to keep asking them until I get the full truth," Katie said defiantly.

"What makes you think I'm lying?" he asked.

"Because that's what you do. Most of the time, anyway," she said, her voice rising. "But you've told me some of the truth, I think? Why not tell it all?"

He smiled slightly, and his eyes gleamed with a flicker of animation.

"It was just an experiment. I was trying to see how far I could go."

"What do you mean?" she asked. She didn't know what he was referring to. Was the conversation with her the experiment? Or had that been when he'd encountered Josie?

Katie's head was spinning. There was no way to tell if he was goading her, or admitting to fact.

"Experimenting with fear. The sensation. The horror. The beauty. I wanted to know how far I could go. I wanted to see how far a person could be pushed, and what she'd do for her life. It was all just an experiment. One I never repeated."

"What are you talking about?" Katie whispered. She felt horror fill her at his words.

"I'm sure you know," he said, his voice soft and mocking.

"Was this with Josie?" Katie demanded again. She felt so confused and was developing a serious headache.

He shrugged casually, as if she'd been asking him the time of day.

She stared at him, wondering if she would break. Wondering if she had the courage to stand up to him, to challenge him, when every word she spoke to him and that she heard in return, felt as if it was shattering her.

It was a test, she realized. He was trying to intimidate her with his words, to see how she would react to him.

"Why should I believe you?" she demanded.

"Maybe you shouldn't. I choose what to say. You'll never find out what really happened. That's between me – and her."

She stared at him, feeling her anger and frustration grow. She wanted to batter him with words, to force him to confess, but she knew this man was a true psychopath, and immune to psychological pressure.

But then, his expression changed, as if he'd lost patience with the game. Or, perhaps, he was worried that she'd come too close to understanding more.

"Stop wasting my time. Stop asking these questions," he threatened her.

"Why is that?" Now she felt a strange coldness inside.

"You have no idea what I'm capable of," he said, without a hint of emotion. "Do you want to find out the hard way? Because I can make it happen. Even from in here. I know who you are, and where you are. You wait and see."

Abruptly, Katie felt as if she was going to throw up. She looked away, breathing hard, and heard his triumphant laugh.

But then, one of the guards spoke, his voice loud and angry.

"That's a threat! You just gave an officer of the law a direct threat."

He glanced at his colleague.

"That's it. That's enough. Combined with your other offenses over the past week, we're putting you in solitary."

"No!" Everton protested. For a moment, finally, she saw the cracks in the evil, complacent facade. For a moment she heard genuine emotion in his words, and the fear of being banished to solitary.

"Come back in a couple of weeks," the officer told Katie. "Until then, this guy's earned what he just got."

They stood up, unfastened his handcuffs from the chair, and led him out, snarling and protesting.

Katie stood up. She felt emotionally wrung out, shattered by the toll it had taken to face this man. Another guard was waiting at the gate to escort her back to the prison entrance.

As she reached it, her phone rang. It was Scott on the line.

Katie guessed he might be calling to find out if she'd made progress with Everton, since she'd told him why she wanted the time off. But as soon as she heard the tone of his voice, she realized it was more serious.

"Katie, we have an urgent case called in," he said. "A fugitive has fled into our territory. He's a killer and extremely dangerous. We don't yet have an ID on him, but I have a sketchy description of him which I'll forward to you."

"I'll be back there as soon as I can," Katie said. "My flight leaves in two hours."

But Scott had other plans.

"From the evidence, this killer has already crossed the border from northern Montana into British Columbia. There's no time to waste as he's leaving a trail of murders behind him. His latest victim is an FBI officer. He set a trap for him at his old lodgings in Colorado."

Katie drew in a horrified breath at this news.

"Leblanc's already on a plane to Kelowna, British Columbia. So I need you to take the first available flight there," Scott continued, his voice hard. "This man must be stopped, as soon as possible, or who knows how many lives will be lost."

CHAPTER FIVE

Leblanc sat in the lobby of the hotel in Kelowna, waiting anxiously for Katie Winter to walk in, so that they could get started with their newest case.

The lobby was a sleek, impersonal place, with deep gray carpeting and pale gray furniture. He was seated on a couch facing the door. The hotel was a five-minute walk from the airport and car hire companies, and her flight had landed fifteen minutes ago, so he expected her at any time.

He felt a mix of emotions about seeing her again.

He was looking forward to working with her, but this was a dangerous case that had already claimed the life of a seasoned FBI agent.

That made Leblanc apprehensive. It brought home to him exactly how much risk their job entailed, and how exposed he and his partner were on a regular basis, with the types of cases they handled. Again, he thought of the decisions he needed to make, and his old life back in Paris.

He caught a glimpse of himself in the mirror on the far side of the wall. Close-cropped dark hair, olive skin, dark eyes, and an expression that seemed to convey that at the age of thirty-five, the weight of the world was on his shoulders.

He shrugged his shoulders, as if trying to rid himself of the pressure he felt. He knew part of it was of his own causing. He was complicating his own life by being undecided. But both he and Katie had their demons to face.

He was going to help her with hers. But he hadn't yet confided in her what his darkest thoughts were about his own. How could he? Even he couldn't bear to face them.

A moment later, he saw her walking into the lobby, wearing black pants and a burgundy coat. She had a purposeful walk that was different from the others who passed in and out of the lobby. The sight of her made his heart leap a little.

That told him something, Leblanc admitted, as he jumped to his feet.

She strode over to him, wheeling a small carry-on behind her.

They shook hands. Her grasp felt warm and firm. He wasn't sure he wanted to shake hands with her. After what they'd been through on previous cases, a hug felt more in order.

But Katie was protective of her personal space. Leblanc knew that, for her, a handshake set clearer boundaries. Boundaries neither of them was ready to overstep, or even challenge.

"I've booked us a meeting room upstairs," he said. "Shall we go there immediately? We can conference-call with Scott and he'll take us through the case."

"That sounds good," Katie replied.

They took the elevator to the second floor, and walked down the corridor to their meeting room. It was small, with a round table and a window that overlooked one of the airport runways. Beyond, was a view of pale, snowy land that Leblanc knew would be lush and green in a couple more months.

A water cooler sat in one corner, and there was tea, coffee, and snacks on the shelf next to it.

He led the way into the room and they both took their seats.

Leblanc set his briefcase on the table, took out his laptop, and pulled the screen in front of him. He attached his cell phone to the cord, so they could conference-call Scott, and then powered up the laptop, noticing it was eleven a.m.

A few moments later, their boss answered the call.

"Leblanc. Winter. I'm glad you could get there so quick," Scott said.

"What are the facts so far?" Katie asked, her voice clear and level. Leblanc was always impressed by the calmness and focus she brought to her work. It was seldom that she lost balance or control.

"The suspect was living off the grid in Colorado for a while. A couple of local residents knew him by sight, but kept their distance. There's talk that he was a hunter or a trapper, and a few people think he went by the name of Wolfe, but it might be a nickname or an assumed name. His real identity is not known."

"Do we have a definite link to the crimes?" Katie asked.

"Yes. He was observed by one witness building a trap. The witness didn't understand what he was seeing at the time and only came forward later. Then another witness saw him leaving the scene of the most recent crime. He saw Wolfe standing and looking down into the trap."

"And it's definitely the same person building the traps, and watching afterward?"

"Yes. The descriptions are close enough that we can confirm they are of the same man. And based on our examinations of the traps, we have enough evidence to conclude he's intentionally setting them in places where human foot traffic passes, to kill humans."

"Did the witness follow him when he left?" Leblanc asked.

"Yes. It was too late to help the victim, but the witness followed Wolfe to the shack, and then ran back to his car to call the police."

"Brave man," Leblanc observed.

"Yes. A fit, brave, and lucky man. It's thanks to him we have the information we need. I'll send you the report he made to the police, which gives a description of Wolfe. But by the time the local FBI swooped in, he'd fled, leaving the place trapped, and unfortunately we lost an experienced agent there."

They were silent for a moment. Leblanc saw Katie shake her head sadly. Losing a good agent was a huge blow.

"How did they track him so far north?" Leblanc asked.

"He stole a car from a truck stop a few miles from his shack. The owner was in the shop at the time and saw him climb in the car. He described him as a tall man with a dense, bushy beard, wearing furs. Which ties in with the other witness descriptions of Wolfe."

"Go on?" Leblanc felt captivated by the account of their newest challenge.

"The car was picked up on cameras, heading on Interstate 97 toward northwestern Montana, and was found abandoned at the stop just before the border, north of Oroville. The closest town on the Canadian side is Osoyoos."

Leblanc had his laptop out and was watching as Scott interactively used the map, pointing out the highways and towns that had come up so far on the police reports.

They did indeed show a route heading north.

"It's very likely, given the above, that he's already crossed the border on foot and is heading north. He's dressed for the cold, equipped for it, and will probably be looking to either hide out, or set up a base."

Leblanc glanced at Katie, seeing the same determination in her eyes that he felt.

Time was of the essence here.

"How did he construct the traps?" Katie asked.

"He is creative and dangerous in the way he works. He uses local materials. He's previously used steel rebar, a bear trap, wire, and makes use of the natural terrain that channels people onto a path, in much the same way that someone might do when setting up a snare."

Leblanc shook his head. He knew he should be inured to the evil in these killers, but it shocked him every time.

"Where do you want to start?" Scott said.

"Probably, the best place will be the truck stops that are closest to Osoyoos," Katie said.

Leblanc could see that she had an idea in mind.

"I'll wait for your updates, and will send through any further information immediately," Scott agreed.

They disconnected the call and left the meeting room.

"I'm hoping we might find some CCTV footage of him, in one or other of the truck stops," Katie explained, as they rushed downstairs.

The wintry air was cold, and the sun hadn't yet risen far enough to warm the day.

They walked to the black SUV Leblanc had hired earlier, parked near the entrance, and then climbed in.

Leblanc got behind the wheel, and they drove out of the airport. Programming his GPS, he was reminded all over again how vast the distances were. They'd gotten to the closest possible international airport, but even so, Osoyoos was a two-hour drive away.

"You think examining the footage will be enough of a reason to go there?" Leblanc asked, wondering if this was the best use of their time.

Katie frowned. "That's not the only reason. I think Wolfe will start doing what he knows how to do. What he's good at. He'll trap and kill to get what he wants, so we need to get close to his presumed location. Before too long, I think we're going to find another victim."

CHAPTER SIX

The north was calling to Wolfe. He felt its pull. The open spaces were waiting for him. Spaces where he could be safe, with no eyes on him and no surveillance in place. This was where he needed to be. Far north.

He knew that they had been watching him. That he was being followed. He felt it, like a constant static in his head, muddling his thoughts and creating a sense of panic.

As he trudged through the snow, he picked up a rhythm to try and calm himself.

Ten paces, then glance behind him.

Ten paces, then look to the sides.

He'd been moving through the snow since dawn. He was exhausted, but knew he had to keep going, because they were coming after him.

He'd only just fled in time after realizing that he'd been seen, and they were on his trail. It chilled him to realize how close he had come to being captured at last. Now, he had to push through his tiredness and put some distance between himself and them.

Ten paces, then look behind him.

Ten paces, then look to the sides.

The furs felt heavy on his body. His thick beard was flecked with snow. His hands, in thin, tattered gloves, were cold, but he needed to be able to work with them and a heavy covering was unwieldy.

He wasn't safe yet, but he would be. As soon as he'd gotten enough of a lead on them, he could relax. He had to get clear. His survival depended on it.

Ten paces, turn and look behind him.

He looked back, and could see the snow churned up by his feet. He was leaving a clear trail. If a plane flew overhead, he'd be spotted.

Even though he'd already checked the sky, and there was no plane overhead, they might come for him in a helicopter.

He wasn't sure how many wanted him dead, but he guessed that their numbers had grown. By now, there might be quite a few of them. Maybe even a large group, working together.

He moved forward again, climbing the ridge, unhappy about his footprints, anxious to change his location fast.

Wolfe stopped, listened. He was experienced in scoping out the terrain, identifying the sights and sounds that could help him. He needed to make his next move. He couldn't be predictable. What he needed to do next must be unexpected and surprising, to keep them on the back foot.

He could hear a distant hum. An engine of some kind. Staring around, he assessed where the noise was coming from.

It had to be close, because the engine was loud, but he couldn't see anything, in his field of vision.

There was the sound, louder now, and he realized what it was. It was a snowmobile. Someone was riding it, over the hill ahead.

The snowmobile represented movement. It was his chance at speed. He needed to take advantage of it, to get away from them.

And he could set a trap. He hadn't had time to gather much equipment, but he had been able to grab a few items as he'd fled. What he had would be enough.

His mind settled as he crept toward the ridge, his paranoia briefly calming as he focused on the hunt ahead.

Wolfe loved to hunt. He understood it. It was all about predicting where the quarry would be. What the movements would be. Then, skill and patience took care of the rest.

His mind flashed back briefly to the days when it had only been animals. Hares, foxes, sometimes bigger and more dangerous prey.

He'd learned how to make and set several kinds of traps. He'd been well taught and had become extremely skilled. But he'd also devised his own traps, unique and deadly. He'd realized his talent in this direction. He was made to do this. There wasn't any prey that he couldn't catch, if he put his mind to it.

Then his mind flashed back to that moment, a few months ago now, when he'd seen the human, dead and bled out in the bear trap he'd set.

His mind had seemed to bend, and reality had warped, as the terrible realization had sunk in. Guilt and shock had filled him, but then his thoughts had shifted, and he had understood that this man must have been following him. That was why he'd landed in the trap. It could have gone very badly for Wolfe if he hadn't.

Since then, he'd made sure to be constantly vigilant. He'd scoured the area, but it hadn't been enough. He knew they'd been watching him, that they were pinpointing him, and had set more traps to keep them away.

Suddenly, Wolfe was dragged out of his memories and back to the moment by the sound of the snowmobile, going around the long track again.

The rider was definitely alone. There was time to get ahead of him.

Wolfe set about his plan, moving swiftly.

First, he checked behind him again. Then, he hurried over the ridge, running through the snow, his breath clouding the air. He observed the tracks made by the snowmobile as he looked for the perfect place to work.

There it was, ahead. A place where the track narrowed and ran between two sturdy trees. He could feel that location calling to him, beckoning him. It was the right place and where he needed to be.

As Wolfe moved in, his gaze roamed constantly. He could never afford to be careless. His eyes were tuned to pick up the slightest hint of movement, and his ears were straining for any sound of voices, or dogs, or helicopters.

He had to be careful, to ensure that this trap was set up in the way he wanted it, in the right place, to trigger fast and effectively.

He worked hard, feeling confident in his job. He needed to be able to move freely, so he shed the furs that were weighing him down. He had a kind of hide-coat underneath. It was made of tough but stretchy leather, so that he could freely move his arms

The trees provided overhead protection so they couldn't see him from above, with their helicopters and drones. He was so calm that, as he worked, he whistled softly through his teeth.

There, it was done.

He was pleased by how invisible it looked. From a distance, nobody would be able to see it. Particularly not a snowmobile rider, wrapped in heavy clothing and goggles.

Did he have the height right? That would be important.

He checked again. Yes, the height was fine.

Whistling again, his mind abuzz with ideas, Wolfe donned his furs again. He had forgotten they were watching him. Perhaps, at times like this, he was invisible to them. Perhaps preparing the traps gave him that power, just as setting the skulls around his cabin had done. For a while, anyway.

Wolfe turned and began walking, quickly and silently, looking for the best place to become invisible again, and hide.

As he did, the paranoia returned, worse than before.

This had to work! It had to. His life, his everything, was now at stake.

The next few minutes would be critical.

Wolfe knew that the snowmobile would be coming soon. The engine noise became louder and louder, throbbing in his ears.

There he was. He saw him, a hint of movement through the trees.

Wolfe knew that this was it, the moment that would decide his future and allow for the next phase of his escape. The snowmobile was racing toward him, and he was ready with his trap.

CHAPTER SEVEN

Nearly two hours after leaving the hotel, Katie and Leblanc sped up to the truck stop that was closest to the town of Osoyoos, near the US-Canadian border.

Hoping this would provide them with some useful leads, Katie slowed as she reached the small set of signposts and buildings. A few trucks were stopped in the parking lane. The place looked snowy, cold, and quiet.

They climbed out. The cold hit her, chilling her face and catching in her throat.

"You think he would have come here, and not gone to the stop on the US side?" Leblanc asked her.

"I think his overriding aim would be to cross the border undetected. He wouldn't have wanted to cause potential trouble until he was safely across," she explained.

"Why is that?" Leblanc asked.

He didn't sound combative, merely curious. She explained, as they walked over the snow, heading for the small general store ahead.

"I've been trying to get into his head, based on what we know of him so far."

"And what are the main points?"

"He's a trapper. He lives off the grid. He definitely does not want to be around people. It's possible he's paranoid and actually feels threatened by them. So he would want to flee, until he was at a place where he didn't feel at risk from border patrol. Then he would seek to regroup and regain what he left behind."

Katie felt, as she spoke, that she was on the right track. This was who he was. The problem was that it made him a dangerous and an elusive person to hunt down.

"What would he be looking to regain?" Leblanc asked as they reached the store's doorway.

"Shelter. Transport. Food. Money. Weapons and supplies. Based on his mindset, I would think transport would be high on his list, because he will want to be mobile and to move fast. But to obtain it, he might need other things. Perhaps he would have come here, looking for them."

"Weapons?"

She shook her head.

"He doesn't seem to like confronting people. He seems to prefer indirect contact. He's a trapper. But that makes him even more dangerous."

She strode into the store.

It was a basic place. A few shelves stacked with provisions. But also, there were other supplies. Katie went and took a look at the hardware shelf.

This was the place that she thought this man would be drawn to if he'd come in.

On the shelves, she saw hammers and axes, hatchets. There were also knives. Sharp ones. Utility knives, hunting knives. There were coils of wire and bolt cutters and screwdrivers.

Katie glanced up.

To her relief, there was a camera directed at this shelf, where probably the costliest items in the small store were kept.

"We need to take a look at this. Perhaps we can pick up if he was here," she said, pointing.

"The footage from the camera might show him more clearly," Leblanc agreed. He followed her to the front of the store, where she approached the man behind the counter, a friendly looking man in his fifties, wearing a knit cap and scarf.

"Good morning. We need your help urgently," she said sternly.

The man's smile disappeared as he took them in.

"Sure, what's going on?"

She produced her ID. "FBI. We need to pull your footage."

"Why?" He gaped at her, concerned.

"We're looking for someone," she said. "And we think he came in here. Based on what we know of him, he would probably have spent some time at your hardware shelf."

He nodded. "Of course. Was this recent?"

"It would have been this morning."

Looking flustered, the man led the way to a back room, where there was a bank of small screens.

"How far back do you want to go?" he asked.

33

"About two or three hours. We're looking for a man who's quite distinctive. Perhaps you noticed him? Tall, broad shouldered, wearing heavy clothing and furs. Probably with a beard."

Katie knew he could easily have changed his appearance by cutting it, but didn't think he would easily give up the layers of hair and clothing that she thought provided armor against the world.

"Ah, I think I do remember that guy," the man behind the counter said. "He's not an unusual type. We get quite a few of that sort of person coming in here. The hunters, the people off grid, who like to live independently. But there were only a couple of them here today."

"Can you find him for us?"

He nodded confidently. "Yes. Let me go back a couple of hours."

Focusing carefully on the screen, he scrolled back through the footage, before pointing at the small screen.

"There we are," he said.

Katie leaned forward as the store owner pulled up the images.

"What did he do when he came in here?" Leblanc asked. "Did you notice anything unusual about him?"

"He didn't buy anything. I remember thinking he was just browsing, taking a walk after filling up with gas. Again, not unusual. Not everyone buys from here. Some just come in to stretch their legs and have a look around."

Katie peered intently at the flickering screen as the footage rolled back.

"There," the man said. "I'm not sure if this is your guy, but it seems the most likely."

The image was blurry, but it was definitely the man that fitted the description they had been given. Wearing a thick coat, his beard obscuring his features, he peered down at the hardware selection.

Katie and Leblanc looked at each other. She felt a thrill of adrenaline that they had, most probably, their first actual sight of the killer.

"The camera's at a good angle. Can you zoom in on his face?" she asked.

The store attendant did, and they both studied the screen, looking at the grainy image. He had long hair that looked dark in color. His beard was dark, heavy, and covered most of his face.

Katie felt frustrated that the hair and beard was providing a very effective cover, making it difficult for them to see his features clearly.

"He's not a youngster," Leblanc said thoughtfully. She could tell he was also doing his best to piece together what he could from the grainy image. "Not old, but he doesn't look to be in his twenties."

"No, I don't think he is," Katie agreed. "In his thirties or even forties, perhaps."

"You need to check your stock," Leblanc told the man in a stern voice. "It's likely that some items have gone missing. It might be helpful to us if you could tell us what they are."

The man went pale, staring at the footage.

"You think he was a shoplifter? A thief? That would be unusual," he said, sounding concerned. "Most of the guys like that, they're honest."

"Not this one," Katie agreed sadly.

Sure enough, as they observed the footage, they saw the man was groping at his pockets, shifting his body around. If he hadn't taken anything, Katie would have been shocked.

"I'll check the stock lists immediately," the owner agreed.

"Can you zoom in farther on that last section of film?" she asked, hoping they might pick up more detail.

The man tried, but the picture became totally unclear.

However, Katie noticed something as he fumbled in his pocket.

A tiny glimmer seemed to materialize for a moment on the gray floor.

"What's that?" she asked.

She and Leblanc stared at each other.

"I've got no idea," Leblanc said. "But it looks as if he might have dropped something."

At this stage, any evidence would be helpful. Turning, they rushed through to the main store, heading for the hardware shelf.

Bending down, she checked under the shelf, and her eyes narrowed as she saw what was there.

"It's a British Columbia ID card," she said, and heard Leblanc murmur in surprise.

"That would be lucky for us," he said, in tones of carefully suppressed excitement.

"If he was fumbling with his pockets, stashing stolen items away, trying not to draw attention to himself, he could have dropped it without even realizing," Katie said.

She crouched down and, using a piece of cardboard, teased the card onto a piece of paper. This card was laminated and would hold prints, which could be important. They couldn't touch it but needed to see it before sending it off to forensics.

They stared down at the small card, lying on the white sheet.

The picture was grainy and slightly out of focus. However, it showed a clean-shaven man with a shaved head, and a blank expression, dark eyes, and a heavy brow.

The name on the card was Eric Sands.

"Eric Sands," Leblanc echoed. "Let's get his address."

He quickly messaged the details on the card through to Scott.

"If he's Canadian, what was he doing in Colorado?" Leblanc asked.

"Nothing to stop him traveling further south for a while," Katie said. "He clearly does not have much respect for borders, and knows how to move around and live in the wild."

"But is it the same guy?"

"It's impossible to tell if the features match," Katie said thoughtfully.

"A man with such a heavy beard, such long hair, could have grown it out as a disguise."

"Yes. This ID card is a few years old. So it's possible," Katie agreed. "What's his age?"

Leblanc checked. "Forty-one. So he's within the ballpark we were guessing at."

Meanwhile the store attendant had been checking through the stock.

"We do have some items missing," he said.

"What are they?" Katie could hear the concern in her own voice.

"Two coils of wire. Two sets of wire cutters. A hunting knife, and a couple of screwdrivers and pliers," he said. "There might be more. On a basic check, that's what I've picked up. It's extremely unusual. Out here, most times, the stock balances well. And like I said, the type of person who is likely to steal things is not that type. You get to know after a while who to look out for, and you keep an eye when they walk in."

Katie nodded grimly.

"He's planning on setting up some sort of an operation," she said to Leblanc. "He must be going to trap in order to get what he needs. And we have no idea where he might have headed, once he left this store."

The extent of the danger, and the damage this man could do, made her feel cold inside.

At that moment, Leblanc's phone buzzed.

"I have an address from Scott," Leblanc said, sounding excited. "Eric Sands lives just outside Vancouver."

"That's a five hour drive away," Katie estimated.

"I'll check with Scott if there's a helicopter available. That would get us there within an hour, hopefully," Leblanc suggested.

"The helicopter would be the better option. We need to get there as fast as we can," Katie said. "We desperately need a confirmed ID on him. If this guy is Eric Sands, then his family or friends might be able to fill in the gaps. In fact, for all we know, he might be heading toward his old home, looking for shelter - or revenge."

CHAPTER EIGHT

This time of the year, the morning sun was dazzlingly bright. It blazed ahead of Adam Grieg as he rode the snowmobile at full tilt along the track and he narrowed his eyes against the blinding light.

He was in a temper today, riding faster than usual, testing himself against the unpredictable terrain and slippery snow.

Bosses! He was sick of being micromanaged and nitpicked. Attention to detail? You could shove it!

Now that he'd had the time to get his head around his situation, his outrage was at a peak. He knew about sales and marketing. He had experience. He'd been working for this company two full months, but they treated him like some new recruit, making him jump through hoops. Well, he was a player, here. A star. They could deal with him in a proper manner.

Their doubts about his skills and his ability to work with the team - he'd seen where that was leading. He was a brilliant salesperson. An asset to the team. But if they didn't treat him right, he was going to quit.

Adam's face was set in a grim line, his lips tight together. They could do what they liked, the lot of them. But he was taking control. Somehow.

He was sick of the delays, the meetings, the demands on his time. He was sick of being fed a load of corporate crap about customer relations, company ethics, and marketing the brand. What did he care about that? He knew how to bring the deals in.

And the so-called managers, the people trying to tell him what to do - he was sick to death of their superior attitudes.

He had been glad to get out of the office, glad to feel the cold air on his face, to see the world flash by in a blur of dazzling white and blue, and the shadows that leaped out of the trees.

He was a natural salesperson, a dealmaker, a man of action.

"I've always done it my way," he'd told them. "Why should I change?"

Of course, they hadn't listened and had only come down on him about being late for an appointment the previous day. Banging on about professionalism, like he hadn't actually written that textbook himself.

He was going for a ride to clear his head after their criticism. He wasn't going to do his rounds this afternoon. Not after that meeting and what they had said. If they were lucky, he'd start the client visits tomorrow. This was the construction industry, after all. Not like the materials had an expiration date on them, right? He needed to be in a good mood to clinch the deals. Today had been an annoying waste of time.

To his left, the rocky terrain was steep and stony. To his right, it sloped away into an ice-covered valley. It was a challenging route, even for an experienced rider.

He was fairly experienced, and could control the snowmobile just fine, but he'd never driven it this fast before.

He hadn't dared. But today he was in a mood for a challenge. He was riding the route again, and at a higher speed.

Ahead of him, he could see the terrain - the gently undulating land - begin to even out. He'd be out of this forest soon. Then he'd begin to climb, up to the ridge. Despite his best efforts not to, he couldn't help but glance down at the valley. It looked somehow treacherous.

He knew how rocky this section of the track was, and couldn't help a flicker of fear that it was about to give way and he would hurtle down into the depths.

The snowmobile rattled and roared its way across the frozen land. It seemed to be the only living thing out here, in its own small world.

Pines flashed past, looming up beside him, reaching for an icy sky. Then a hard turn to the right, and he was heading into a steep dip.

He gripped the handlebars tighter, and his heart leaped into his mouth. He should slow down, be more careful. But then again, he could test his limits.

With a roar of the engine, he swerved through the dip. He'd made it without slowing, and was heading for the narrowest part of the track, where the pines flanked the snowy path, their branches silhouetted against the blaze of the sun.

And something else. A tiny thread, the darkest line across the sun, with tiny knots along its length.

What was it?

His first thought was a spider web. But a spider web wasn't a single strand?

His thoughts lagged way behind his speed, and even as the first confused ideas entered his mind - even as he thought he should duck to avoid it - Adam reached the line.

It felt as if a giant hand grabbed him by his neck.

His head wrenched to the side. He felt a sharp, choking pain. He was flung backward off the snowmobile, somersaulting into the snow as the vehicle veered away, its speed bleeding off before it thudded into a tree.

Snow showered down on him as he somersaulted down onto the track.

Pain and confusion filled him.

What had happened?

He was breathing hard, but somehow, it didn't feel as if the air was getting to where it should be. He didn't know if he could move his arms and legs. He was in utter shock.

But, as the world came slowly into focus, Adam realized to his horror that he was lying in a spreading pool of blood.

Where was it from?

Amid the throbbing pain of his body, the sharp agony in his neck told him something was very wrong.

He lifted a trembling, gloved hand to his neck and stared down in dismay as he lowered it again.

His glove was covered in blood. It was gushing from his neck.

He'd gotten tangled up in wire, and it must have had barbs on it. It had literally ripped open his throat, Adam realized, as ghastly reality descended.

This was a bad one. Real bad. There was no stopping this. He didn't know how.

He could die here.

"Help!" he croaked, or tried to croak, even though he knew the plea was pointless, in this vast, empty space. His throat was burning. "Help!"

He stared down at the snow around him, staring at the bright redness of the blood.

His phone! He should call for help, and fast, because his body was going into shock. Already, he felt his strength draining away. Where was his phone?

Groping for it in his pocket, Adam couldn't find it. It must have fallen out as he tumbled. He couldn't see it anywhere.

A shower of red drops spattered down on the snow. Forcing his legs to obey him, he tried to stand up. But his knees couldn't take his weight. They buckled, and he sank back into the bloodied snow.

Panic began to clench his heart. He had to get up. He couldn't stay here! If he couldn't find his phone, then he had to get back onto the snowmobile and head for the hospital.

He gritted his teeth, and forced himself to try again. This time he managed to get to his knees, before sinking back down.

And then, the shadows of the trees moved and he looked up, squinting as a tall man appeared, his bulky form cutting out the low, dazzling sun. He heard his footsteps, heavy and distinct, crunching through the snow.

"Help!" Adam groaned again. "Please, help me. I need a hospital."

The man must be able to see that he was laying in a pool of his own blood! The snow was crimson.

But he was doing nothing. Just watching.

He wasn't even saying a word. This tall, big, bearded man was standing there in absolute silence.

Adam stared at him in confusion, and as he did, the man nodded slowly, raising a finger to his lips, as if he wanted Adam to hush.

Then he turned to stare at the snowmobile. The snowmobile was dented, but it seemed undamaged. The man walked toward it.

Reaching the snowmobile, he put his big hands on it, lifted and turned it. He checked it over, and then he turned and looked back at Adam, his eyes dark and inscrutable.

Adam felt a sense of total disbelief.

The man was stealing his snowmobile, and he was going to let him die. He was going to let him bleed to death in the snow.

This man must have caused this. Created this scenario.

As his mind struggled to reach the impossible, unthinkable conclusion, Adam felt the last of his strength ebb away.

He slumped onto his back, staring up at the brilliant sky, listening to the sounds of the snowmobile as it started up and roared away.

CHAPTER NINE

Katie stared out of the chopper window, watching as Vancouver appeared on the horizon. They'd been able to use a helicopter from the local police department, which shortened the timeframe, to her relief. Before they left, she had handed in the ID card so that it could be sent to forensics to check for fingerprints.

Now, just thirty minutes after takeoff, they were nearing their destination. It was a long way to go, but knowing the killer's correct identity would be a huge step forward. Without an ID for the man, she felt as if they were fumbling around in the dark.

They were heading to the most westerly police department and would then use one of the RCMP's vehicles to drive to Eric Sands's last recorded address in suburban Vancouver, a few miles from this police department.

As the chopper swooped in to land, Katie checked the address again.

4 Egret Avenue. What would she find there? Tension felt coiled inside her. The hunt for this man was on.

The chopper touched down, the blades slowing. Removing her earphones and unfastening her seatbelt, Katie saw the SUV was already waiting in the parking lot adjacent to the helipad.

Climbing out, the cold wind hit her, but at least the sun was shining and it had been a smooth flight.

She walked toward the SUV and saw the driver's door open. The man inside scrambled out. He was holding a coffee mug and a GPS screen was mounted on the dashboard.

"Good afternoon. Chilly weather," the man said, shivering in the wind that was slicing across the open paving. "I'm Constable Nathan. You must be from the task force."

"Agents Winter and Leblanc," Katie introduced them.

"Good to meet you and thank you for organizing the ride for us," Leblanc added.

"We understand this suspect is highly dangerous. Do you think he could be in the vicinity yet?"

"If he stole a car, he could be here by now, yes," Leblanc said. "If not, at least we may get an ID on him, which will be very helpful."

"If you require any backup, there's a radio in the vehicle, or else here's my number." He handed them a card. "We'll deploy officers if you need them. It's in everyone's interest that this criminal is caught as soon as possible."

"Thank you," Leblanc said.

"I have the address programmed in the GPS. So you're ready to go. Good luck," he said, giving a brief nod before hurrying back to the police station.

They got in, Katie automatically taking the position behind the wheel.

She pulled out and hit the road, driving fast to Eric Sands's address.

The tension was building. What would they find?

Would this be his place of residence, or would there at least be clues to his current whereabouts?

The salt air filled her nostrils, and the scenic streets of suburban Vancouver sped by her windows. Katie barely noticed the homes, trees, and parks. Her mind was totally focused on what would play out when they arrived. Had Eric Sands stolen a vehicle and headed for his home address? Or had he gone elsewhere?

They took the turnoff for Egret Avenue. The road was narrower, the houses single-family homes rather than the closely packed condos in downtown. It was a mostly residential area.

"There it is," Leblanc said, his voice tight.

Katie nodded. She could see the number on the mailbox. She pulled over and parked on the side of the road.

They climbed out of the SUV. Side by side, they strode up to the front door and hammered on it.

Her ears strained. She could hear someone approaching from inside.

The door opened and she stared at a woman, who looked to be in her late thirties. She was wearing jeans and a jacket, and had a stressed expression.

"Can I help?" she asked.

"Ms. Sands?" Leblanc asked.

The woman looked confused. "What? No, I'm Lee Brown. This is my house."

Her eyes widened as Leblanc showed her his badge. "W-what brings you here?"

"We're looking for information on a man called Eric Sands. Do you know him?" Katie said.

"Yes, I do. But he's not here."

"Where is he now, Lee?" Leblanc pressed.

"I don't know. Look, he does stay here sometimes, but we're separating. I'm filing for a divorce. If he's caused any trouble, it's not my fault."

"Did he cause you any trouble?" Katie asked. It sounded as if he might have done so. Perhaps Lee could provide some background that might explain the killings, and the move to Colorado.

"He got into a lot of debt recently," Lee said, shaking her head sadly.

Debt? Katie felt surprised. That wasn't what she'd expected the other woman might say.

"Does he work?" Leblanc asked.

"He's not employed at the moment. He lost his job about three months ago, and now he's doing odd jobs for people."

"Does he have a beard?" Katie asked, wanting to know if the suspect description matched up.

"Yes. He has a big, bushy beard. He grew it out about two years ago."

That checked a box, she thought.

"Has he been out of town recently?"

"He was away for a couple of weeks, last month. I know he was in the States, but I don't know where."

Katie's doubt grew as she remembered that the suspect they were seeking seemed to have been based in Colorado for longer than that. But, as she stared hard at Lee, she didn't trust that this woman was telling the full truth. She thought she was looking to avoid trouble.

"Are you sure you don't know where he is now?"

Her guess was right. Lee shifted her feet uneasily, looking down at the floor.

"You won't get into trouble, I promise. We're looking to check his whereabouts and see if he is connected with a recent crime," Katie reassured her.

Lee frowned. "He's been doing some transport for people. To try and keep up with the payments on his truck. He might be packing things up at the Watsons' house down the road. It's the one on the corner, with the green gate. But please don't tell him I told you. I really don't want to rat him out."

Katie nodded. "We won't. If he asks, we'll say we found out another way."

They climbed back in the car and headed down the road.

Approaching the corner, Katie saw an old Mazda pickup parked outside.

A man was offloading goods. As they drew closer, she saw that his face was similar to the man they were seeking. He had a bushy beard. But there was an immediate and glaring problem.

Eric Sands was probably five foot four. He was a short man, though strongly built. But no way did he match the witness reports of the breadth and height of their suspect.

Katie decided immediately that she was going to change tack. This was almost certainly not their guy, but she needed to know how he'd managed to lose his ID, and whether he'd been in contact with the suspect at the time.

She pulled up alongside the truck and climbed out.

"Good morning. Mr. Sands?"

He nodded. "That's me."

"We're investigating an incident, and we think you might know something that could help."

By then Leblanc had also hopped out of the car and approached the truck. On the same page as Katie already, he said, "You mind if we ask some questions?"

"Sure. Go ahead," he said. He didn't look at all guilty, Katie thought. He looked open and willing to help, if rather confused.

"Did you lose any ID recently?"

He frowned.

"Yes, I did. I was transporting some furniture to Rock Creek yesterday. I stopped at one of the gas stations to repack the load and I only realized afterward that there was a hole in my coat pocket. I think that's where it must have fallen out as it was gone by the time I reached the customer. I thought of going back but I guessed the chances of finding it were just about nonexistent. I'm applying for a new one tomorrow."

Katie nodded. Disappointing as it was, it was clear this was not their suspect.

"Did you see anyone at the truck stop?" Leblanc asked. "Notice anyone watching you?"

Eric shrugged. "It was very early in the morning and still dark. I was the only person there, as far as I could see."

"Thank you," Katie said.

This was disappointing and frustrating, but it seemed that Wolfe must have opportunistically picked up the ID card. Then he had used it, subtly, to make it look as if he had dropped it by accident. That move had sent them in the wrong direction.

That was a seriously smart and sneaky move, Katie acknowledged. It had been so plausibly done, and showed a high ability to pre-plan and predict. She knew that she could not afford to underestimate this man in the future, because he was a master of trickery.

As she and Leblanc trudged back to the car, her phone rang.

She saw, with a sinking heart, that it was Scott on the line.

"There's been another murder," he said flatly as soon as she picked up. "A few miles north of Osoyoos. I'm organizing a pickup with the police chopper again. You need to get there as fast as you can."

CHAPTER TEN

This crime scene was all the way out in the wilderness, Leblanc thought, as Katie powered the unmarked police vehicle forward on the road heading out of Osoyoos. They'd climbed out of the helicopter ten minutes ago, and were now driving out of town along a side road that led into a wild, forested area.

The remoteness of the scene gave him a small crumb of comfort, because there was no way they could have predicted where he would strike. Going to Vancouver had been the wrong decision. He was angry that they'd been outwitted and had spent so many hours pursuing the wrong lead. Leblanc consoled himself by thinking that there would have been no right decision that might have prevented this crime. And at least, with a chopper ride there and back, they'd wasted the least possible amount of time.

The road wound through a forest, over a bridge and alongside a frozen lake, before winding its way into snowy fields.

Flashing lights ahead signaled that a police roadblock was in place. Katie slowed the vehicle to a crawl, and stopped at the roadblock.

"You need to head that way," the policewoman at the roadblock pointed. In the snow, the road was nothing more than a double track.

Katie swung right and followed it, bumping over the uneven ground. The track wound left and right through the fields and then, ahead, near a cluster of trees, the double-track petered out entirely.

A police van was parked there, together with an ambulance, their lights bright in the deep shadows of the trees.

Katie parked behind the van and Leblanc climbed out.

They trudged up to the trees, where two RMCP officers were waiting, together with a couple of civilians standing near their snowmobiles. The snowmobile riders looked utterly shocked. Leblanc guessed they must have found the body.

Behind them, the ambulance started up, and jolted away down the track.

"Good afternoon," Leblanc greeted the group. "Leblanc and Winter from the special task force."

The RCMP officer closest to them stepped forward.

47

"I'm Sergeant Atkins," he said. "Thanks for your help in this." He also looked shocked, Leblanc saw.

"What happened?" Katie asked.

"The victim was killed by a piece of wire. Barbed wire, strung tightly between two trees. Take a look. I've never seen anything like it. We've already loaded up his body, but the bloodstains are still there, and you can see the photos we took."

Leblanc followed Katie as she led the way around to the crime scene.

There, to his consternation, he saw a length of barbed wire, stretching between two trees, across the snowmobile track.

There were deep marks in the snow, as if someone had fallen heavily, and a couple of yards away from the wire, the snow was stained deep crimson. Leblanc felt horrified as he saw how brutally effective this trap had been.

"He didn't stand a chance," he muttered, shivering.

"These gentlemen found him lying there, about an hour and a half ago. They were riding the same route," Atkins said.

"Who is the victim?" Leblanc asked.

"Adam Grieg. They knew him slightly. Said he's lived in town for a few years now. He did have his ID on him, and his phone was half buried in the snow near the track. So, this seems to have been a grab-and-run crime, with the aim of getting his snowmobile."

"And the death? Did he break his neck?"

The officer looked even more distressed. "No. It seems he must have just bled out. That's what the paramedics said, anyway."

He clamped his lips shut, as if unwilling to theorize more about the bloody end this victim had met.

Leblanc could read the man's face, and knew he was thinking the same thing.

There was something deeply disturbing about this killing. Anger surged in Leblanc as he thought about how cowardly it was. How this man set up a lethal trap, knowing his victim would suffer.

And then he must have watched, he thought with a shiver. What kind of person would cold-bloodedly observe as the trap triggered, simply waiting for his victim to die?

He knew that Katie had ventured far further into that realm of investigation than he had. A glimpse into this mindset was more than he wanted, but he knew he needed to try and understand his actions.

After all, they were pursuing this man into the remote wilderness and would need to predict what he might do.

Leblanc turned to the closer of the two snowmobile riders, who was hugging himself, looking cold and distressed.

"I can't believe anyone would do such a thing, sir," he blurted out to Leblanc. "If he hadn't been lying under that wire, we'd have run into it ourselves. It was almost invisible against the snow, and exactly at neck height."

"Did you see anyone else on the trail?" Leblanc asked, wondering if they could have sighted the killer departing. "Anyone waiting nearby?"

"No, it was just us. We were the only ones out there."

"Was the victim's snowmobile anywhere in sight?"

"No. No snowmobile. I guess whoever did this must have stolen it. You can see where it crashed into the tree, but it's gone."

"We need to take a look at the tracks," Katie said, her voice urgent.

Leblanc knew she was right. The tracks would undoubtedly point the way to where the killer had fled.

Cautiously, he stepped forward, seeing the gouges in the snow where the snowmobile, without its rider, had veered and plunged to the left. It had hit a tree, but not hard, he guessed. It might be dented, but it had clearly been drivable. Dents would be something to look out for.

And then, he saw deep footprints in the snow.

He imagined how Wolfe must have calmly walked over to the machine, mounted up, and driven off.

Ice cold, Leblanc thought, with something approaching horror.

"Boot size? Do we have an estimate?" he asked, taking refuge in facts to blot out his own imagination.

"Size twelve," one of the police confirmed. "We've taken pictures."

Leblanc tried to piece together in his mind what had played out, as he stared down at the tracks.

The killer had moved the snowmobile, shifting it away from the trees. He guessed that was what had happened. He stepped out, gazing at the snow, and saw what he was looking for.

The tracks swung left, and took a new route, heading out to the northwest. That was where he had gone, with his stolen vehicle. Over the snow. Disappearing into the wilderness.

Katie was looking at the tracks heading away from the crime scene, and Leblanc could see she was thinking the same thing.

He had an idea.

"Can we borrow one of your snowmobiles?" he asked the two riders.

They looked startled. "You want to ride out there?" the closer one asked uneasily.

Katie nodded. "We need to see where he fled."

"That could be very dangerous."

"We'll be careful."

"You can use my machine. But - what if you ride into another trap?"

Leblanc shrugged. "We'll be on the lookout for that, and won't take any risks."

"We'll take care," Katie said. "We'll ride together. There's enough space on this seat for two of us."

Leblanc nodded. Two would be better than one, in this case.

"I'll radio for local backup, and for a police helicopter to join the search also," the officer said. Leblanc felt reassured that they would not be alone for long.

But they would be for now, and would need to be extremely cautious.

Leblanc swung his leg onto the snowmobile and patted the seat behind him. Katie stepped onto the back of the snowmobile.

Leblanc could feel the vibration of the engine through the seat, and smell the cold exhaust.

He hoped this journey would go safely. And he hoped that it would get results.

"Come on," Katie encouraged him. "Let's go track this killer."

CHAPTER ELEVEN

Sitting behind Leblanc as the snowmobile powered over the terrain, Katie leaned to the side, peering at the tracks ahead. Two sets of eyes were better than one as she scoured the area ahead for any signs of Wolfe.

Katie was keeping a close watch out for any traps he might have set up.

So far, she didn't see any, but she had no doubt there could be some. The killer might still have some tricks up his sleeve.

As the snowmobile raced on, its engine a loud, vibrating roar, Katie thought of how that same engine noise could alert a man lying in wait for them.

She was keenly aware of the danger, and of the fact that there was no backup as yet.

The cold was biting. She felt it through her clothes, seeping into her skin, making her shiver.

She wrapped her arms around Leblanc, pressing closer to get herself out of the wind.

Moments later, they were riding past a small circle of trees, and heading across the flat trough of deeper snow.

"He can't have gone too far," Katie shouted, thinking aloud. "Not with a stolen snowmobile and leaving visible tracks. I reckon he wanted to get a lead on us. I don't think he will keep it for long."

"I think you're right," Leblanc said. She felt him tense as he pushed the machine harder, trying to maximize its speed, because every moment counted if the journey was going to be short.

This was the closest they had been, physically, she thought suddenly, her mind veering in an unexpected direction. And it was the closest she had been to anyone for a while, she realized.

She allowed herself, for just a moment, to enjoy the feel of her arms wrapped around him, his warmth against her. But enough of that now, she told herself firmly.

The cold was numbing her face and throat, and she could feel the wind biting at her hands. The engine raced and roared, and the machine was slowing as it hit deeper snowdrifts.

Leblanc slowed down, allowing their eyes more time to scan the area ahead.

As they forged forward again, Katie was trying to understand what kind of mindset the killer was in.

First, he had set up his "murder wire." And then he had made his escape with the snowmobile. It had been seamless and without any hitches.

That made her wonder, was Wolfe confident in what he was doing? Or was he driven by fear? Katie was hoping that it was the latter. A killer who was driven by fear would be reckless, and make mistakes.

So far, though, he had showed a very high level of resourcefulness. He was able to think on his feet. She saw him as someone who was not going to be deterred easily.

Is that the kind of man we're up against, she wondered, watching the snowy landscape race by. It was a disturbing thought, but one she needed to consider.

Katie held her breath as they approached a trail junction where the trees loomed in on either side, and exhaled in relief as they cleared it safely. The adrenaline coursing through her veins made her feel alive.

Katie thought again about Wolfe. He was ruthless and fearless. But what was the vision behind this act? Did he have a plan, a destination in mind? Was he driving toward some remote hideout, where he could safely hide away from arrest?

Peering ahead, she saw what looked like a forested area.

Was that where Wolfe was heading? It would be impossible to drive a snowmobile through the woods. Katie felt a flicker of unease.

Leblanc slowed right down again. In the uneven snow, he'd lost the tracks. This was Katie's forte. She stared at the glittering snow, looking for the signs she needed.

"He's heading for those trees," she shouted above the roar of the engine to Leblanc, pointing ahead, to the rugged area of woodland. "Go slightly left. You'll pick them up ahead."

Leblanc nodded, increasing his speed again.

"He seems to be heading straight for the forest," he shouted.

Katie sensed, in her gut, that Wolfe was not panicking. He was being calm, and thinking clearly. As she'd thought, he had ridden toward a destination where he could lose anyone who was following.

Leblanc slowed once again as they approached the trees. The tracks ran alongside the forest.

"We'll go carefully here, and keep a close eye out for any trouble," Leblanc shouted.

"Okay," Katie said.

She turned all her attention to the trees ahead, knowing they could be hiding something, or could be concealing another trap.

And then as they crested a small rise, she saw it, at exactly the same time she felt Leblanc tense.

A splash of yellow ahead.

"It's the snowmobile," she shouted.

There it was, parked in full sight, at the edge of the woods.

Leblanc slowed right down. They climbed off and approached the last few yards cautiously, on foot.

It had a dent in the front, she noticed. Without a doubt, this was the machine that had been stolen. Now, where was Wolfe?

She felt a sudden, overpowering sense of threat and stared around her.

Was he watching them right now? Or was he hiding, waiting for their next move before he made his countermove in turn?

She felt certain he would not have waited, and was long gone, but her uneasiness remained. There was something about that snowmobile's bright, obvious presence that made her feel deeply suspicious.

"No tracks," Leblanc said, sounding disappointed. This side of the woods, the snow was thin and sparse. Looking between the trees, Katie could see a hiking trail winding its way into the forest, but it was impossible to discern any fresh footprints among the clumpy snow, chunks of ice, pine needles and leaves.

"He must have joined the hiking trail."

She looked around. There was no other way he could have gone. Beyond, the woods were thick and impenetrable. Undoubtedly, he had taken this trail.

But staring into the forest, she saw the trail forked. One section went deeper into the woods, and the other veered right, heading up a steep slope near the edge of the forest.

Which direction had he chosen?

Leblanc got onto the radio.

"We've found the snowmobile. He's gone forward on foot. You can come and collect the other machine."

Katie stared from left to right along the track. Turning back, she noticed that Leblanc was examining the snowmobile more closely.

"There's something here. Under the seat. I think he dropped something when he ran," Leblanc said.

He bent down, peering at the machine, reaching out a hand.

"What's that?" he said, sounding surprised.

At that moment, Katie's dread solidified.

Wolfe wouldn't have left evidence. He would not have made such a mistake. The last ID card he'd left behind had thrown them onto the wrong track, wasting precious hours which enabled him to kill again. This was nothing more than another, more dangerous, piece of misdirection.

She heard the tiniest sound, a hissing noise, coming from the snowmobile's engine.

She realized what this meant and leaped to Leblanc, grabbing his jacket, tugging him away as hard as she could.

"It's a trap! Get away! He's wired it to explode!"

CHAPTER TWELVE

Katie sprawled on the ground, rolling away, even as the hissing intensified and a bright, loud blast filled the world.

There was a flash of fire, and a sudden puff of smoke, as the engine exploded.

A shockwave sent her reeling. The snowmobile shot up in the air, and she could hear the whoosh of the debris and the parts flying through the air.

Something heavy slammed into her from behind, and she sprawled further forward in the snow.

Silence descended, as if a switch had been thrown, and the world stood still, just for a moment.

Then she heard Leblanc groaning.

Her head was still spinning. Cautiously, she raised it and looked around, dreading what she might see.

Leblanc was lying on his back on the ground, and he was coughing. He looked shaken and disoriented, but to her intense relief, he seemed unhurt.

If he'd been closer, if he'd stayed near the machine while it blew, things would have been very different.

The snowmobile's engine was a blackened, twisted wreck. The propeller was a mangled mess of twisted, bent steel. Nearby, the remains of the seat were still smoldering.

"Are you sure you're okay?" she asked, anxiety flaring as he coughed loudly. If she hadn't pulled him away, the snowmobile would have exploded in his face. Undoubtedly, it would have killed him.

Leblanc struggled to his feet, staring at the burning snowmobile, his face full of shock.

"I'm fine," he muttered. "And you?"

Her hands and legs were bruised, and a piece of the snowmobile had whacked her in the back of the thigh, but otherwise, she was unhurt.

She looked at her hands, and saw black smears on them.

"I'm okay, too," she said.

"That was a close call. I - I can't believe what just happened there."

Katie nodded. She was shaking with reaction. This man, Wolfe, was cunning, ferocious, and had an uncanny ability to think ahead.

Katie, on the other hand, had not been thinking straight. She had been overconfident. She had thought they were all done with surprises.

Like prey lured into an ambush, they had almost been taken down by the tidbit of evidence he'd stealthily left.

Not only had the stolen snowmobile provided his escape, it had then been converted into a trap, to destroy the evidence, and to kill whoever followed.

Wolfe had planned ahead, thinking through each step of the plan, in a calm and calculating way. He'd done it with surprising speed, and it had nearly worked.

He had allowed them to find the snowmobile, and he had allowed them to go near enough to see what looked like evidence in the foot well. That had been his first step. The second step had been to blow up the snowmobile, to kill them both.

It was a bold move, made with confidence. He had gambled that they wouldn't be paying attention to the engine, and that they would be too curious to suspect a trap.

Had it not been for Katie's instincts, screaming a warning to her at the last possible moment, things could have ended very differently.

But enough of that now. There was no more time to piece together what had happened, when they needed to move forward.

"We have to get after him," Katie said.

"Agreed," Leblanc nodded. "The more time he has to construct these things, the worse it's going to go for us."

Quickly, Katie got on the radio and messaged in their location.

The radio crackled in reply.

"We're sending backup," the RCMP officer stated. "We'll have a helicopter there in half an hour, and we're deploying some officers to search the forest."

"Copy," Katie said. "We'll search the local area in the meantime. Be very careful. He just wired the stolen snowmobile to explode. We escaped the blast, but only just. The loaned snowmobile is undamaged, so you can return it to the owner, but don't let him come near this area. This suspect is highly dangerous."

Katie took a deep breath as she considered her options, which had drastically narrowed down now that they knew how fast he could work. There was literally not a minute to waste. The first and most important information they needed was to find out which way he had gone.

Every moment counted in their pursuit of the fleeing man. They had already lost too much time.

"Shall we take a look in different directions?" she said.

"Why?" Leblanc asked, alarmed. "Right now? After what just happened?"

He glanced back at the still-smoldering snowmobile, which was sending a plume of dark smoke up into the sky.

Katie knew the smoke would alert Wolfe that they had triggered his trap.

"We need to cover more ground. He might be moving fast. If we split up and search, we have double the chance of picking up his tracks. We don't have to go too far. Just do basic reconnaissance. And we can stay in touch."

She could see his expression change as he considered her logic. He was worried about splitting up, but he also knew it was the sensible thing to do.

Leblanc nodded, reluctantly.

"Okay. Let's do that," he said.

They headed into the forest, with Katie taking the lead. The trees were quiet. The woods seemed peaceful. But she knew they were not. They would be in danger from the minute they started tracking him.

It was a case of risk versus benefit, and the benefit of finding which way he had gone was greater than the risk of operating individually – just barely.

"If you have any trouble, or something seems out of the ordinary, get in touch straight away and let me know," Leblanc said.

"I will," she agreed.

"Which way do you want to search?" Leblanc asked.

"I'll take the left," Katie said, deciding on the route that led deeper into the woods.

Leblanc gave her a nod and they set off, each in a different direction.

The trail was a narrow track of snow, winding like a pale ribbon through the trees. Never had Katie felt under so much threat when pursuing a suspect. It felt like a lethal game of hide and seek, and she didn't have a good feeling about it.

She was as exposed as if she'd been walking down a well-lit city street, and she was as threatened as if she'd been walking down a dark alleyway.

Wolfe was smart, cunning, and ruthless. He'd set a trap for them already and he could have been setting more.

No matter how carefully she moved, Wolfe could be watching her.

He could be observing her right now. Her heart beat faster at the thought.

She glanced around her, but all she could see was the snowy track stretching off into the distance.

She couldn't see Wolfe lurking in the woods. But that didn't matter. He could be out there, and he had an ambush prepared.

The trees were close-set on either side, like a prison. There were many places for him to hide. The underbrush was thick, and the trees tall and solid. The air temperature was falling as the sun sank lower.

Katie glanced around her uneasily. She focused on the trees, trying to look past them, deeper into the forest. But she could see nothing unusual, nor hear anything beyond the faint rustle of the wind through the treetops, and the crackling of branches as they swayed slightly in the breeze.

The breeze was picking up. Just what she didn't need. It would help Wolfe more than her.

She took a deep breath, and began to follow the trail, staring down for any sign of his footprints but seeing nothing. Stay alert, she thought. Concentrate. Be constantly aware.

Every step could mean her death, and already, it was getting darker in these thick and impenetrable woods.

Katie wavered. Should she turn back? Perhaps this was the wrong way. Perhaps splitting up had been a bad idea.

But then, she saw what looked like a partial print ahead.

She'd almost given up too soon! Katie rushed up to it, knowing she must be on the right path, and feeling renewed determination flare inside her.

CHAPTER THIRTEEN

As she reached the footprint, Katie saw it clearly. One large boot print, that looked to be the right size, heading into the woods. It wasn't clear enough for her to see the tread. But at least it was a sign.

Then she began second-guessing herself. Was this print too obvious? Was it a red herring? Had he made this footprint purposely, to look like he was going this way, and then doubled back? She knew she couldn't trust anything he left as evidence.

But perhaps he genuinely had been hurrying to get away.

Barely daring to breathe, Katie moved along the track carefully, her senses prickling, staring down for any sign of boot prints. She knew they would be less clear here, in the sheltered woods, with the carpet of pine needles obscuring the track and only sporadic patches of snow.

She was very aware she was working against the clock, and every minute counted.

But as she paced forward, her thoughts kept going back to what had happened a few minutes ago. Leblanc had so nearly been killed. Katie found herself feeling short of breath as she replayed that moment.

She'd nearly lost him, and she was surprised by how emotional that made her feel.

Was she becoming too involved, she wondered. Was she starting to care for her partner too much?

The thought made her uncomfortable. Because she'd learned that people she cared for could turn their back on her, ghost her, cut her from their lives. Like her parents had done.

Even though she knew she had to protect herself from hurt, she couldn't suppress that feeling of trust, that warmth inside her, when she thought about Leblanc.

Impatiently, Katie shook her head, trying to clear it. She could not afford distraction. She had to get her emotions under control, clear her mind and concentrate on what she was doing. This was not the time to allow her thoughts to wander. Not when a moment's inattention might get her killed.

Putting her feelings aside firmly, Katie focused on the task ahead.

The trail led through the trees, winding along a gentle downward slope.

As she walked, she tried to think about Wolfe's mind. That was where she needed to focus her energies. On what he would expect her to do, and how he might try to get a jump on her.

But she couldn't imagine what move he might make next.

She considered that, but she couldn't see a way to stay ahead of him. At this point, he was completely unpredictable, an unknown entity. And it was frustratingly difficult to track him when every footprint was hidden beneath the thick carpet of pine needles.

Every time she saw a spot of snow which looked clear, she focused carefully for any sign of his tracks.

There was something. She caught her breath, staring down as she saw another large, clear boot print visible.

This was visual confirmation he'd followed this route. Hope surged inside her as she moved on down the trail, searching for more boot prints.

Further along, she found partial but distinct prints in a drift of snow, a few paces farther. She bent and looked at them, trying to see the pattern of the sole. Even though she felt excited and resolute, she also felt increasingly anxious. These prints were recent, and she might be close to the killer.

She followed the trail, slowly, carefully.

Then, to her surprise, in a drift of snow, she saw that there were two sets of footprints. Clear and distinct.

Two people had walked this way?

Katie wasn't sure the new prints were the same size, but now it felt too late to turn back and check. However, this cast doubt on whether the original footfall had been Wolfe's. Perhaps a group of hikers had walked through.

Then Katie frowned. There were now at least three sets visible, and the snow was trodden and trampled.

Peering closely at the jumbled prints, she decided three people had walked up this way and then turned back. It could only be some sort of search party.

That still didn't explain the original, single footprint she had seen. Thinking back, she was sure that one had been larger. So what had happened? Had the original print belonged to Wolfe? If so, where had he gone? Perhaps hearing others had made him take a different route, or forge a path through the trees to a different track?

She stopped, listened carefully. The wind was gusting toward her and she heard voices on it.

Men's voices. And she picked up a familiar sound. The crackle of a radio.

Katie moved forward more quickly. The local police must be getting involved in the hunt already. That was good, because it meant more manpower. But it was bad, because since they had approached from this side, they might have obscured any clearer footprints.

And also, this group might not be aware of the most recent developments.

Katie sped up, knowing she needed to warn them to be careful.

"Agent Winter?" a voice called.

"That's me," she called back, not liking that there was now all this noise. This wasn't going to help.

There were a group of three RCMP officers ahead, she saw, as the track veered to the right. They were spread out, picking their way slowly through the trees, making a lot of noise.

"What's going on?" she asked, as she approached them.

"We're following tracks up here. We noticed footprints coming this way, but we can't find any clear traces of them further down."

"And you haven't seen any sign of the suspect?"

"No, ma'am. No sign of him."

At that moment, the officer furthermost from her peered curiously into a tree.

"There's something here. Caught in the branches. Looks like a piece of paper."

"Wait!" Katie shouted, urgency flaring inside her. "Don't touch!"

Too late, she realized what Wolfe must have come down here to do before he vanished into the woods.

But her warning went unheeded. The officer moved forward, and then shouted in surprise, jerking his leg back.

His foot was caught in a noose. A moment later, as if activated by a spring, the wire tightened.

The man screamed as he was jerked off his feet. It wasn't a spring, Katie saw in horror. It was a strong, tall sapling, bent and trapped in wire. Now, with a lashing force, it straightened, carrying the man with it. He was yanked up into the air, dangling upside down. A moment later, his head crashed against the tree trunk with a hideous cracking noise.

Katie felt horror flare inside her. In the blink of an eye, this situation had turned deadly. She wasn't a fearful person, but there was something about the way this killer worked that created a deep and visceral fear.

"Help him! Quick!" Katie shouted, pushing her own terror aside. "But be careful. There could be a second trap!"

She rushed forward, knowing it was dangerous, but needing to save this man's life.

The wire was attached to the tree by a heavy gauge metal hook. She could feel the tension in the wire, and it was hard to move it.

"Hold him up," she asked the other two officers. "If you can take his weight, I'll try and free him."

Unconscious, the man was a dead weight. They did their best, holding him while Katie stood precariously on a nearby tree stump, and fumbled to loosen the wire noose that was biting into his ankle.

There was no way of telling if her weight on the stump would trigger a second trap. How far ahead had he thought and planned? It didn't matter, she knew. An officer's life was now at stake, and she had to try and help, as best she could, suppressing the horrible feeling that she might be pulling an unseen trigger.

Finally, she managed to ease the wire loose and was able to wrestle the loop off his foot.

"Hold him! Let him down," she gasped. Her legs were quivering as she stepped off the stump.

Katie watched anxiously as the other men carefully lowered the injured constable down to the ground.

The man was breathing, but there was a nasty wound on his head that was already bleeding heavily. This was all going so badly wrong, she thought in despair.

"You need to call for backup and get him medevacked out. He might have cracked his skull," she said. "We need an airlift to take him to a hospital immediately. He's not in a good way."

"I'll call it in," one of the officers said. He fumbled with his radio.

The man on the ground was unconscious, leaving Katie standing there, feeling helpless. But she was also aware that she had to get going, because Wolfe was ahead of them, and gaining.

Now that the shock of what had happened was abating, she was able to piece together some facts. The killer had left this trap. He definitely had not gone further or he would have met the police. So he'd created it, and either veered away or retraced his steps.

She'd first thought he must have fled through the undergrowth, but it was thick and heavy. The scenario that made far more sense was that he had doubled back.

That meant he'd gone the other way – and that was the way that Leblanc had chosen.

Had he set a trap in that direction, too, she wondered? And if so, what would happen when Leblanc walked into it?

A chill ran down Katie's spine. She had to warn him.

At that moment, from up the hill in that direction, she heard a faraway shout.

Adrenaline surged inside her as she turned and began sprinting toward the noise, hoping that she would not arrive too late.

CHAPTER FOURTEEN

Leblanc headed along the track, which had a series of steep uphill slopes. He was scrutinizing the terrain carefully, looking for any signs of the heavy, size twelve footprints that would show he was on the killer's trail.

He saw enough, in glimpses, to convince himself he was on the right path. There were scuffs and partial prints every so often. But there were also tangles of undergrowth that had all his instincts flaring, because they could conceal a trap.

There was no way of knowing if the killer had walked into the thicket to hide away, or if he was lying in wait.

Reaching the top of the rise, Leblanc paused, gasping for breath after the steep climb.

The killer couldn't have gotten far, he told himself. He had to force himself to ignore the danger, to just keep on going.

His focus sharpened as he saw a large, snow-covered log ahead. Beyond it, the snow had built up. He drew in a quick breath as he saw there were clear boot prints. The snow beyond was trampled and disturbed.

Shivering, he looked around. Knowing that Wolfe might be close by was not a reassuring thought.

Leblanc drew his gun. He held it with difficulty, as his fingers were still clumsy and numb from the snowmobile ride. His gloves had not been adequate for that intense cold.

Just take it easy and keep calm, he told himself, as he forced himself to keep going, steadily, methodically, checking each step.

He saw another partial print. Feeling encouraged, he moved forward, staying as quiet and alert as he could. After what happened earlier, he had no doubt that he might be walking into a trap himself.

Ahead, he saw more clear prints, leading past a thick bank of bushes.

This was a definite sign. The prints looked further apart, as if whoever had made them might have started to run.

Feeling confident that he was going to gain ground, Leblanc forged up the hill.

But, as he did so, the bushes to his right erupted and a large, bearded man stormed out.

He was probably six-foot-two, with massive shoulders and long, tangled hair that was dark and greasy. A bushy beard obscured his features. Heavy furs were draped over his shoulders. His giant hands were bunched in fists.

Leblanc only registered these impressions for an instant, swinging round, his hand too slow and too numb to use his gun.

The massive man tackled him and his gun flew out of his hand, skittering across the snow and into the undergrowth.

The blow of his fist caught Leblanc so hard in the chest that he was driven back, his breath knocked out of him. He stumbled, and then they were on the ground, rolling over together.

Wolfe was surprisingly fast and impossibly strong. Immediately, Leblanc knew he was fighting for his life.

The man's body was like a coiled spring, ready to unleash. He was an explosion waiting to happen, a man possessed with incredible strength.

He attacked with a flurry of blows that Leblanc parried as best he could, but the blows bruised and jarred him. Wolfe was powerful, far too aggressive, and his attack was ferocious.

It was clear to Leblanc that he was dealing with a rough but brutally talented fighter.

He blocked a blow and ducked instinctively to avoid another, realizing that any punch directed toward his head would be almost certainly fatal, because it would stun him and then the fight would be over. He was not about to let that happen.

He tried to think clearly, to keep his wits while looking for an opening, but the other man was too strong and too fast. He had to twist and squirm to avoid the blows. Wolfe was climbing onto him, all attack, seemingly with no thought to his own defense.

Weirdly, Leblanc sensed that he was terrified in his onslaught. He was fighting like a desperate man.

It took all his strength to parry a blow that was aimed at his thigh.

Leblanc, who had just enough room to maneuver his right arm, used it to punch the killer in the face, forcing him back.

Wolfe flinched, gasping, but then brought his knee up and kicked Leblanc in the chest. He reeled backwards, as the man advanced on him. He was breathing hard. Again, Leblanc thought he looked scared, rather than confident. He suddenly remembered what Katie had said about the possible paranoia.

Perhaps he could use that to his advantage, he suddenly realized.

"Help!" he shouted at the top of his voice. "Bring in the others! I need help here!"

Sure enough, he heard the man gasp harshly.

Seizing the moment, Leblanc dodged another punch and launched a kick at his left knee.

Wolfe was prepared for that, though, and he blocked the kick with his arm, attacking with a wild punch that Leblanc dodged. For sure, he was panicking now.

"Bring in the others!" Leblanc yelled again. "I need backup!"

He felt the man's grip loosen, and he thought he had him.

But then the man whirled and slammed a forearm into Leblanc's face, and Leblanc's head rang with pain.

He staggered and the bearded man started punching him ferociously, as if he was running out of time.

Leblanc managed to use his arms to block a few of the blows, but the killer got through and hammered a blow into his side.

It was as if someone had rammed a baseball bat into him. The pain was shocking. Paralyzing. He followed it up with another blow, and Leblanc reeled back. This attack was relentless and Leblanc was gasping for breath.

Wolfe swung an elbow at his throat, forcing Leblanc to tilt his head back to avoid the blow. He saw his moment and he slammed his fists into the man's stomach, firing blow after blow at the same spot, driving him back.

The killer was momentarily dazed and Leblanc stepped in and slammed a punch into his face.

To his surprise, Wolfe shook his head, unaffected by the blow. Then he launched himself at Leblanc again, snarling in rage. His fingers jutted out, catching Leblanc in the neck so that he choked. His strong hand grabbed Leblanc's ankle and wrenched him sideways. Pain flared in his leg and he yelled aloud, in pain this time.

Even though Leblanc was down, and dizzy with pain, he fought back with all of the strength he had left. He grabbed at the other man's ankle and tugged with all his strength. Finally, he got lucky. Wolfe stumbled over a tree root. He was thrown off balance for a moment and Leblanc landed a solid kick to his left knee.

Wolfe howled in pain and went down.

"Help! Help! Backup needed!" Leblanc yelled again.

But this time, he heard answering shouts from down the path. He heard a man's voice call out, and also the familiar sound of Katie's voice.

He lunged forward, ready to grab the killer, but with a strength that Leblanc could not believe possible, Wolfe wrenched his arm away from Leblanc. He scrambled to his feet and set off at a stumbling run.

Leblanc was enraged. Wolfe was injured, but he was escaping.

He had been so close. He had been so close to catching him.

Leblanc knew he needed to follow, but he couldn't. The fight had destroyed him. His chest was on fire and his arms were quivering from the effort of defending himself against the taller, heavier man who'd fought with the strength of total desperation. Pain lanced through his leg.

But he knew which direction he'd gone. He couldn't let his injuries stop him, and nor could he wait for backup to catch up.

He was going to follow. Even though, injured and weakened, he knew he would be an easy target if he was ambushed again.

With his gun drawn, his breath coming in harsh gasps, Leblanc set off, plunging along the trodden track through the undergrowth with his last remaining strength.

CHAPTER FIFTEEN

Leblanc shouted again as Katie sprinted up the steep hill. Pain was audible in his voice and it constricted her stomach, causing her to redouble her pace as she scaled the brutal uphill.

Behind her pounded one of the three RCMP officers, gasping as he tackled the incline.

"Leblanc?" she called. "Are you there? You okay?"

It was terrifying to know she was pursuing a killer who could swiftly construct deadly traps. Even as she ran, she felt herself holding back inside and scanning her surroundings in fear.

"Leblanc! Where are you?" she shouted again. Desperation lanced through her. This was turning into a nightmare.

This time, a faint answer.

"Over here!"

Katie's heart leapt when she heard the voice. It was weak and breathy, coming from a beaten track off the main path ahead.

She followed it, plunging through the undergrowth, not entirely sure where he was, or even if he was okay. Anxiety surged as she saw him ahead, swinging around to face her. He looked stooped and exhausted and there was a bloody scratch on his face.

"I fought him!" he said breathlessly. "He attacked me. I had him, I had the better of him eventually, but he escaped."

Katie's hand dropped to her gun.

"Where is he now?"

"He fled ahead." His words were laced with pain.

"How far did you follow him?" Katie asked.

"Not far. He got away. He was moving fast."

"Which way? That way?" She pointed ahead to the flattened undergrowth.

Leblanc nodded.

"Don't go," he gasped out. "He's too strong."

But Katie didn't listen. Knowing every second counted, she set off.

She plunged along the rough, trodden track. He'd taken a zigzag route, and she battled to make out where he had fled. She could see little through the undergrowth on either side of her. She paused, listening, but she heard nothing ahead, not a sound.

All she could hear were the two men behind her, panting, struggling to keep up.

She ran further, feeling desperate now, because he'd been so close and yet somehow, he'd gotten away. Her gaze darted right and left. Her heart was racing and she was breathing hard, but she forced herself to keep going.

There was no sight or sound of the man she was chasing.

Katie was beginning to feel the strain of the chase. She was getting tired and she knew this was not some mission in a controlled environment. If something went wrong, it would be bad.

She reached a flat piece of ground where the forest thinned, and the track petered out entirely.

She stopped and looked around her, her chest heaving, gulping for breath. Her side was aching and she bent forward, hands on her knees, taking deep breaths to steady herself. Finally, she had to admit she'd lost him.

Although she guessed she could pick the trail up again, it would take a long time, and the light was fading with every minute that passed. If he'd run headlong, he would be a long way ahead. Leblanc was injured and the other officer was tired. Neither was capable of helping her. And, as she gazed into the murky brush, she saw with a sense of despair that there were too many options ahead. Several tracks branched out into the forest a short distance away. He could have taken any one of them, or else he could simply have made his own way through the less dense undergrowth and not followed a track at all.

Either way, he would be very well hidden by now.

She couldn't keep going.

Her frustration was palpable. She'd been so close to catching him, but now he'd slipped away.

"Damn it, where are you?" she muttered under her breath.

She looked around in every direction, unwilling to give up the fight, still hoping for some indication of where he could have gone.

"He can't have vanished," Leblanc said as he caught up with her, breathing hard. He looked pale with exhaustion. He was slow and unsteady on his feet. She realized to her consternation that the RMCP officer was holding his elbow.

Leblanc was done.

That was it. They could not carry on. Not when her partner was on the point of collapse, and needed medical attention, and when there was a man with a serious head injury waiting to be medevacked further back on the trails.

It was getting dark. Pursuing Wolfe in these circumstances would be misguided at best. At worst, they would set off on a mission where they could be seriously injured or killed.

It went against every instinct she had not to continue the search, but her life, and the lives of the team, were at risk if she carried on. She needed to make the decision and call off this pursuit for now.

It burned her, but it was the safest thing to do. Searching in the dark for a killer who set such cunning traps would put lives at disproportionate risk.

"We'll have to go back," she said, her voice flat and resentful. "We can't carry on through this forest now. It'll soon be too dark, and too risky. We don't have the numbers or the equipment for a night pursuit."

Leblanc nodded. He didn't look happy, but she could see he accepted her logic. It was too dangerous to continue on.

"Let's go," Katie said. Disappointment tore at her.

She took hold of Leblanc's other arm, holding him gently but firmly, because she could only guess how much he was hurting. Then, the three of them turned and stumbled down the hill.

"We can start again at first light," she said, trying to throw some positive perspective into the grim situation.

Leblanc nodded. He still looked pale and exhausted, but he was clearly giving the scenario some thought.

"There's a lot we can still do tonight," he said, his voice strained with the effort of holding himself together.

It was a grueling trek back. All three of them were struggling with exhaustion, and Leblanc was clearly hurt much worse than he was showing. Katie heard him gasp and wince with every step, but he didn't complain.

As they reached the edge of the woods, she heard a trilling noise. From somewhere in his jacket, Leblanc's phone began to ring.

At least that meant they were back in range of cell signal, Katie thought. She wondered if it was Scott calling.

But when Leblanc got his phone out and glanced down at the screen, he killed the call and put his phone away again.

There was the car ahead. The police were waiting to pick them up.

She helped him the rest of the way to the car. The officer at the wheel climbed out and hurried around, ready to help Leblanc inside.

As he reached the car, his phone started ringing again.

"I'd better take it," he muttered.

He limped away, far enough to be out of hearing, and began speaking on the phone.

Katie stared at him curiously.

She could read his body language. It really seemed as if he didn't want her to overhear this call, standing out there in the cold, and watching him made her feel strangely insecure.

Wondering why he was guarding his privacy, she scrambled into the car herself, glad to get into its warmth, and to finally have a chance to sit down. But she couldn't help glancing at him from the window.

What is it, Leblanc? What's going on, Katie wondered.

She didn't want him to feel like he had to hide information from her. But why should he want to? There was nothing she could do but wait and watch as he finished the call.

It troubled her that after all this, they still had any secrets from each other.

Now was not the time. But Katie resolved that as soon as they'd gotten him to the clinic and he'd been checked out, she was going to ask him about that call.

CHAPTER SIXTEEN

They had almost caught him. After years of living free, Wolfe's worst fears had been realized.

He felt battered and bruised as he headed down the track. He'd thought he was far ahead. Never had he dreamed they would come so close to catching him again.

It wasn't supposed to happen. He had isolated himself, planned everything meticulously, and done everything possible to protect himself. And yet, the man had found him.

He shook his head in disbelief, and forced himself to keep walking. He was bruised and sore from the fight. It was not in him to attack, but rather to evade; but at that moment, fear had filled him and he'd had no choice.

They'd been so close. He'd been lucky to escape. He'd almost been captured.

The features of his attacker were etched in his memory. He remembered him. Dark hair, dark eyes. A wiry strength. He'd been a far more lethal adversary than Wolfe had expected. This was the man who was pursuing him, the one he needed to fear the most. Thinking back, he realized this man must have been following him for years. Fragments of memories surfaced in his mind. This man was highly dangerous and now he was closing in. He was the man Wolfe had always been running from.

Perhaps he was law enforcement, he thought with a chill. That meant he was at even more risk.

Wolfe walked in a weaving line through the forest. It wasn't the easiest route, but it was the most undetectable and hard to follow. That was what he needed now. To cover his tracks so they couldn't come after him. That was the first step in his new, immediate plan for safety.

He was now exhausted, but had to keep moving, even though his head was throbbing, his limbs were aching, and every step was an effort.

But he couldn't let this minor discomfort stop him.

He plodded on, his jaw set, his eyes narrowed, gritting his teeth.

He had to keep going, or he'd be caught.

A chill ran through him as he realized that the man had seen his face. He'd seen Wolfe, just as Wolfe had seen him. Now, he was known and could be recognized by the shadowy group that had been tracking him for so long, and had now caught up.

The horror of the thought stopped him in his tracks.

His hands gripped his head as it started to throb in time with his heartbeat. He felt his hair and beard, coarse on his skin.

Hair and beard that would identify him now. He could imagine the "wanted" posters, with his face on them. He would be visible and recognizable from afar.

Wolfe's mind was a blur of terror. This was a disaster. Until now he was sure he'd been able to avoid being seen. Now, he was firmly in their sights.

It had been too much of a risk, coming back here. He shouldn't have done it. He'd been reckless. He'd made a mistake in going to Colorado. He'd hoped that he would escape them there, and for a while he had, but eventually they had been waiting and he'd played right into their hands. Since then, in his efforts to save himself, he'd become increasingly reckless.

He'd made an even bigger mistake trying to get back now. Thanks to his own stupidity, he was going to pay the price.

The hair and beard he'd been so proud of were now a liability.

He needed a new plan, and fast. His original idea would no longer work, not now, not with the risks so high.

Feeling completely cornered, Wolfe realized that he needed to keep moving before he was caught, but that if he kept moving, he would be easily caught.

He took a deep breath. Gathered his nerve. He reminded himself that he was highly skilled. He'd gotten out of tough situations in the past. In fact, his entire past had prepared him for this moment.

Wolfe knew he was intelligent enough to be able to overcome this. A good hunter could think on his feet, and adapt to the changing circumstances. He was a good hunter. He knew how to survive, and how to evade people, and how to move unseen, even though he was a big man.

He'd learned that long ago, when he had been small. His mindset and skills had been formed and honed before he was even old enough to realize the powers that they gave him.

And he had power. That thought encouraged him. Now, he needed to draw on his resources and channel his powers.

Step one: Stop and listen.

It was an easy step to follow. Wolfe stopped. He listened.

He'd grown up in the wild. He'd learned how to listen to the sounds of the forest and identify what caused them. It was a skill he'd had to hone, until he was certain he could hear every sound a human or animal would make, and know if it was a threat.

The sounds that were necessary or important, he paid attention to. The wind in the trees. The leaves rustling. The snapping branches. All those could be important, and all of them might have a bearing on his actions.

Right now, the wind was rising. Howling and rattling in the trees, shaking the leaves so that chunks of snow tumbled to the ground.

The wind was now a factor in his environment. How could he use it to his advantage?

Now that he was calm, his mind was moving at lightning speed, scenarios slotting smoothly into place. He'd thought it would be hard, but now he saw that with a little logic, it could all be very simple.

As he fine-tuned his plans, walking slowly through the forest, Wolfe's mind cleared. He knew what he needed to do, and how he would do it.

Now was the perfect time, as evening was setting in.

Where would be the best place?

He paused at the edge of the woods, surveying the area, seeing the dull glow of lights at sporadic intervals. Spaced far apart, there were tiny shacks and hunting cabins in this part of the wilderness. The lights meant they were occupied.

There was one near the flat gleam of frozen water. He stared at that one for a while.

Then his gaze swung around to another, nestled at the edge of the woods, with a dull glow emanating from the small window.

Softly, he walked toward it, scoping it out to make sure it was, indeed, the right place for him.

He stared at the trees. Moving around, he took a look into the small lean-to behind the house, and nodded in approval when he saw the vehicle there.

That would work. That was the place he would target. It had everything he needed, and now he had a clear strategy of how to act.

The wind howled, rustling the tree branches. Right now, the wind was his friend. It would allow him to set his plans in motion without being overheard.

With the first, second, and third step of his plan clear in his mind, Wolfe headed swiftly for the woods.

Now, the pressure was on, and he needed to work at speed before the police managed to get ahead of him. They could warn people. The man in this cabin might already have been warned.

But Wolfe also knew that the people who lived in these areas were not usually the type to trust the police. They trusted themselves, and their own weapons. Normally individualists, they would prefer to band together, in an informal militia, rather than hand over a situation to law enforcement. Again, that mindset would work in his favor now.

His confidence grew as he began working, quickly and expertly, doing what needed to be done.

It was the perfect time. Striking now would give him all night to gain the distance he needed for safety.

His quarry was waiting. Now all he had to do was to set out the bait.

CHAPTER SEVENTEEN

Leblanc limped out of the local clinic in Cawston, aching all over. He and Katie had been driven there by the police as soon as the injured officer had been airlifted out. She'd gone to get them another unmarked car to use, while he was being attended to by the doctor.

Leblanc knew he was lucky.

He was a mess of bruises and strained muscles and minor scrapes and cuts. But no bones were broken or serious damage done. He knew he would be fine after some rest and time to heal, but he still ached.

And he didn't have time to heal. They were battling with one of the most dangerous cases he'd ever been involved in, and they didn't even know the identity of the man who'd come damn close to killing him.

The wind whipped through his hair. It was picking up. There was some bad weather blowing in, for sure.

There was Katie, waiting in a gray SUV. He headed over to her, trying not to limp visibly as he crossed the road.

From the glimpses he'd had, Leblanc thought that this looked like a pretty town, centered on fruit farming and wine production. It was a place to visit on vacation. Not a place to hole up, knowing that a killer was cutting a swath through the surrounding area.

"Are you okay?" Katie regarded him with concern as he scrambled, with some difficulty, into the car. Trying not to limp hadn't worked so well.

"I'll be fine," Leblanc half-groaned.

He felt furious with himself at having let Wolfe get away. If only he'd been faster with his gun, and not so numb with cold. He'd also been rattled after the explosion. He hadn't been fully focused.

The harsh truth was that he hadn't been on top of his game, hadn't been thinking far enough ahead. Leblanc chastised himself. He'd let Wolfe get the better of him, and despite fighting back, had not been able to overpower him. Instead, he'd vanished into the forest.

Struggling to get a handle on his emotions, Leblanc tried not to be too self-critical. There was no point in it. He'd made a mistake, and he had to learn from it and move on.

That was all. But it was easier said than done.

Katie pulled away.

"I've booked us into the guest suites just down the road. They look very nice," she said.

Leblanc had the distinct impression she was trying to comfort him. But right then, he couldn't accept comfort. Not when he was inwardly screaming at himself for having messed up so badly. He didn't deserve to be comforted.

"I should have done better," he muttered.

Katie glanced over at him.

"It was my fault for suggesting we go opposite ways. I didn't think he'd be waiting to attack. Neither of us could have predicted that. You're still alive and not badly hurt. We'll start again tomorrow. That's enough of an explanation for me," she said firmly.

Leblanc glowered at her.

The guest suites came into view. They did look nice, and there was an eatery next door to them. In this small town, he guessed it must be one of only a couple of places. It was open and bustling.

He knew they needed to go in, get a table, order some food. Recent experience had brutally shown him that he needed all the strength he could get, and couldn't afford to do what he felt like, which was to sulk off to bed without eating.

"Scott was in touch," she said.

"Is he sending backup?" Leblanc asked. They sure needed it.

But Katie shook her head.

"We discussed it, and decided against it."

"Why's that?"

"Anderson is injured. He broke his wrist in a takedown two days ago. And Johnson and Clark are on the other side of the country. They're in the middle of another murder case. Domestic violence. The husband has fled across the border. He doesn't want to pull them off it."

"So we're alone on this one?" Leblanc asked.

"For now," Katie said. "Shall we go in and get some food?"

"Let's do that," Leblanc agreed. He was trying his best to get over himself. Right now, he had to admit, Katie was being the strong one in every way.

As he limped into the restaurant, inhaling the mouthwatering scent of grilled meat, he remembered that phone call earlier.

He didn't want to think about that now. It had been Eloise, phoning from Paris. She'd wanted to chat.

That had not in any way been a business related call. Leblanc had known what it meant. She wanted to take things further. To develop the friendship, and nurture the spark that had been kindled when they'd met over the weekend.

Leblanc sat stiffly down at a table, looking at the menu without really seeing it as he thought back.

In their short conversation, she'd made it plain she would love it if he came over for a visit again soon. She'd also mentioned she might be traveling to Vancouver in the next couple of days for a conference, and if she did, she'd make a stopover to see him.

And now, he thought that maybe, just maybe, he should reciprocate. Maybe he was ready for another relationship. This could be the start of something real and lasting with Eloise.

But he didn't want to think about that now. He felt a surprising sense of guilt, and he didn't need more of that. Not right now, not today. He was still unsure what his emotions really were.

Was he running away from commitment, by flirting with a woman across the ocean in Paris? Perhaps the woman he was developing real feelings for was sitting opposite him now, but he was too afraid of taking it further.

And there were many good reasons for that.

Involvement with a case partner always brought complications, Leblanc knew. It was better not to let it develop. He was here to catch a killer, not to make a new start with a woman.

And he was wary of all the things that could go wrong if he did.

He'd seen many a partnership ruined because of such complications, and he didn't want to risk his future with the task force team because he got involved with Katie.

There were excellent reasons not to get involved.

Maybe he should go to Paris for a visit instead. Just as soon as he had caught the killer.

Thoughts of the prison, and Hugo Gagnon, loomed in his mind again, providing another layer of complexity to his motives that he really didn't want to think about. He stood up.

"I'll get the food," he said. "What do you want?"

"Burger and salad sounds good. I'll get the drinks," Katie said.

Leblanc headed over to the counter. The menu was basic, but the food looked good.

"Two burgers with fries, and a chicken salad, please," he said. That covered all eventualities. He paid, and went back to the table where Katie was arranging two beers and a bottle of water.

He sat down. Stiffly. Hurting all over.

"Who was calling you earlier?" she said in a tone that was interested, but also deceptively casual.

As if she cared, but didn't want him to know.

He had thought she was going to ask him about that phone call. From the moment he'd turned away to answer it, he'd sensed her curiosity. Having been investigation partners for a few months, they were in tune with each other's feelings now.

How he wanted to lie to her. But he knew that would lead him down a very dark road. He was not ready to do that. No way could he break her trust that way.

"It was an ex-colleague, back in Paris," Leblanc said. "I went there over the weekend. It was the two-year anniversary of Cecile's death. I caught up with my old team."

It wasn't the whole truth. But it was as far as he could go. Even so, guilt twisted inside him.

He took a gulp of beer, hoping to deaden the pain that now flared on all levels, physical and emotional.

Leblanc had the definite impression that, despite his best efforts, he was getting into a romantic situation that was becoming far too complicated.

He'd avoided telling his partner the whole truth. He was suppressing his feelings for her. He wasn't even acknowledging what his real motives were for flirting with Eloise, or what he wanted from her.

All this, while the most dangerous killer they had yet hunted was still at large, and would be seeking refuge, disguise, weapons, and who knew what else.

Leblanc dreaded what the next few hours would bring.

The waitress brought the food and he dug in. Grumpy he might be, but his body was desperate for the calories and his stomach growled as he bit into the burger.

For a while they ate in silence. Leblanc hungrily devoured his food, aware that Katie was doing the same.

Then, when he had demolished all his fries, half the salad, and his burger was nearly finished, a thought occurred to him.

"Are we going to go out again after this? And are the police still searching?"

Katie shook her head. "No, and no."

Immediately, Leblanc frowned. Tension flared between them. He felt ready for an argument. Just because he was hurt, he wasn't ready to step down for the night. And why had the police been called off? It sounded as if she'd decided on that.

"Why did you make that decision? Can't you see it's wrong?"

He glared at her, gathering all his resources for a major argument.

CHAPTER EIGHTEEN

It was time for hard truths, Katie knew, as she sat in the small diner, looking across the table at Leblanc. He was angry, withdrawn, in a bad mood with himself and the world. She suspected there were things going on in his head that he wasn't telling her, and that made her worried.

For now, though, she had to explain her decision, and do so calmly, because she didn't want a fight.

She'd seen what Wolfe had done to Leblanc, a tough, experienced officer. She'd seen the devious cunning he'd used in setting his traps.

That had forced her to make a tough, but necessary, call.

"I discussed it with the local RCMP while you were getting checked out," she said. "We agreed to pull the teams off the ground search. They're continuing with the helicopter surveillance for another hour. The wind is picking up fast, so that will soon be too dangerous. But until it's light, it's too risky for anyone to be out on foot. I can't risk other lives. Not against someone who operates the way Wolfe does."

"You're saying this because he got the better of me?" he said, glowering at her. "That's not enough of a reason."

She shook her head. She could see he wasn't ready to admit that he was in no shape for a manhunt.

"He's not beaten, not yet. He'll be regrouping as we are speaking. And we might have a long way to go before we catch him. Plus, the weather's not on our side. There's a gale blowing in tonight. That will create movement and noise, and make it impossible for the search party to be properly alert. It increases the chances that he could trap them, or they could miss something important."

"We should be out there, on the ground, looking for him," Leblanc insisted. "Now, while we have the chance."

"We'll be out there looking for him in a few hours," she said. "But it's too dangerous to do so now. If he's hurt you, what's to stop him doing the same to a patrol or a tracker? The man's already killed multiple times. He sets lethal traps, and darkness would give him a huge advantage. I can't put others at such high risk."

"You think he's too much for us? We're trained. We're professional. We could go."

"I know that," Katie said. "But we're not going to catch him by chasing after him blindly. He's a hunter. He can read the terrain. He can disappear, and he knows how to hide from sight."

"I still think it's wrong," he grumbled, looking away from her, as if he was talking to himself.

"Risk versus benefits," she reminded him. "The risk is too great."

"I think otherwise," Leblanc said, and he sounded bleak. Pushing his empty plate away, he rose to his feet, and she followed suit.

"I'm going to get some rest," he snapped.

He got to his feet and limped out of the eatery.

Katie watched him go, feeling deeply concerned.

She knew some of what was bothering him. But she felt sure he was not telling her everything. It wasn't just the decision she'd made. Other issues were gnawing at him. She could tell.

Walking out of the diner, Katie crossed the road to the guest suites, and headed up the stairs to her room on the upper floor.

The room was decorated in bright, cheerful turquoise and cream. It was a step up from the utilitarian motels they usually ended up in. She wasn't feeling particularly cheerful, however.

Closing the door, she took her phone and called the local RCMP offices.

"Is that Officer Mills?" she asked.

"Mills here," the officer in charge replied. "We've done what you asked, Agent. All the search teams have stood down. The helicopter will land soon. The wind's dangerous now."

He paused for a moment. "Is there anything else we could do?"

"We need to warn people," Katie said. "I know you got onto that earlier, but we could put out another set of messages, to alert the local population that there is a killer at large, and people need to take care."

"We did get onto that earlier. We radioed the local cops in nearby towns, and asked them to contact the locals. A lot of these people are out on their own but they do have groups, online chats, networks, and the like."

"That's helpful," Katie said.

"We're connecting with the local groups, the hunting networks, the smaller villages, and communities. We're trying to do what we can. But as you know, it's hard to police the wilderness."

"I understand," Katie said.

"What about tomorrow morning? What's the plan?"

She thought about their strategy.

"First thing tomorrow, please send your team out to all the lodges, the cabins, the small dwellings within a mile or two of the forest where we lost Wolfe. I think we should do a morning check-up. He might have targeted one of those people and stolen something – a vehicle, a snowmobile. If your team can do the rounds as soon as it's light, that might give us a start."

"Good idea. We'll get going at six a.m.," Mills said. "I sure hope there are no casualties or deaths tonight, but you're right. If he does strike tonight, we need to know, or we will end up days behind him."

Feeling heavy hearted at her inability to prevent what might happen, Katie ended the call, and lay on the bed. She had a few hours to rest, and knew she needed to be fresh, because tomorrow was likely to be tough.

But her mind was abuzz with a multitude of thoughts. In the end, she just lay there and stared at the ceiling, feeling edgy and unsettled, and trying to clear her mind.

She didn't feel like she'd made the right call. Her instincts were screaming at her to go hunting, like Leblanc said. It was hard to think rationally and to stick to what she knew were the correct protocols given the risk.

Firmly, Katie closed her eyes, deciding she would force herself to sleep.

Of course, as soon as she did that, Josie was there. Memories of her twin surged, and yet again, she felt the pain, the uncertainty, the trauma of not knowing what had happened to her.

Did her parents know something more?

Were there secrets surrounding Josie's disappearance that had not been told?

Her mind returned to Everton, now in solitary as a result of his threats to her. He had not wanted to go there. It was the first sign she'd seen that he was actually human, and could experience fear himself.

Would a few days in solitary have an effect? Would it prompt Everton to tell what he knew? Or would he blame her and either refuse to talk, or lie to punish her? Katie knew that she hadn't caused him to go to solitary. His own behavior had gotten him sent there, and the threats to her had simply been the final straw.

She hoped that it would work in her favor, especially if she was able to interview him again, after his stint there. With any luck, the prison would allow her to visit him as soon as he was moved back. Perhaps he would have something to say to her at last.

She lay awake on the bed, worrying, thinking over and over again about what could have happened, her mind going in circles. Suddenly, she wondered what she would have done if she had been in Josie's place, confronted by Charles Everton. Weighing up the possibilities, Katie reached the same conclusion.

She, too, would have begged for her life, and tried to save herself.

What did that mean? She had no idea.

Yet again, she tried to push the whirling, tormented thoughts from her mind. The last thing she needed was to be delving into the past when she needed to be focused completely on the present.

They had a killer to catch, and she had to think about how she could lure him from hiding.

First thing in the morning, Katie decided, she was going to map out his route so far. Perhaps there would be a pattern to his flight, and they could predict where he would be moving next.

CHAPTER NINETEEN

Ben Bouchard put his phone away. He was sick of the chatter, the messages, the endless stream of information and communication. Out here, in his cabin by the woods, he wanted to be alone. But on that bright screen, the world still intruded, baying for his attention.

He'd lived in Vancouver for thirty years of his life. Now, he'd moved out into the wilderness through choice. To be away from all of the noise, the irritations.

And yet, they had somehow followed him here, impinging on his peace.

Community groups. Police notifications. Apps. Occasional messages from telesales people, even though he was now fully off the grid and didn't need them and told them to go to hell. It was as if they still demanded his time.

Bouchard didn't want to be part of the online hive. He didn't want to be part of a society where everyone was constantly monitoring everyone else.

He had always been a loner, even before he had broken his ties with the world. He was now content to live alone in his cabin, to be left alone by others.

It was the way he liked it.

The only contact he had with people was when he needed to have them come out to do work and maintain the place, or when he needed to buy supplies and equipment.

As long as he had the money to survive, he didn't need anyone.

But the technology had gotten more and more intrusive, more and more demanding. It had wormed its way into his life, his space, his privacy. He found it controlling and it was exactly the opposite of what he wanted.

The phone in his pocket buzzed again.

He was tired of the frustration and the irritation, and the knowledge that, no matter how far he ran from society, it was still there, just not in a form he could see.

He was sick of being at other people's beck and call. He should really throw his phone away, break all ties with the world, but occasionally, he did need the damned thing.

Curiosity getting the better of him, he reached into his pocket and pulled out the phone. Glancing at the screen, he saw that it was another community message. Probably a warning about something. Most likely, the wind. He knew about the wind for himself and didn't need to look at the text.

He'd read it tomorrow, Ben decided, getting up to put another log on the fire. He couldn't be bothered now. Technology was the enemy. It was destroying society, destroying the planet, destroying everything. It was a conduit for evil, a tool for annihilation.

It was a very windy night. The strong breeze wailed outside, rattling the windowpanes, and shifting the timbers on the roof. It sounded like a wild beast, howling to get inside.

That was the problem with living on the edge of the forest. The wind screamed like a demon through the trees.

And, at that moment, there was a knock on the door.

He couldn't help it.

He felt a visceral surge of fright at the noise, so loud and unexpected.

And so impossible, since he was miles from anywhere and there were no other cabins within easy walking distance.

Then he sighed. Probably some lost tourist, someone wanting directions, some idiot who'd taken the wrong turn out hunting and blundered through the woods, getting totally lost.

Or else, perhaps he'd misheard, and it was just a stray branch, blown by the worsening wind and thumping against the door.

"Who's there?" he called, placing the log in the correct position on the fire. A surge of light and heat rewarded him.

No answer. Of course.

He opened the door.

There was no one there.

It was pitch black outside. He looked around, but couldn't see a thing except the wild, wailing night.

Frowning, because he felt spooked, despite himself, Ben closed the door again. He walked back to his chair, but before he could sit, the knock came again, hard and insistent.

Definitely not a stray branch. This was purposeful.

He walked over to the window, and looked out. He couldn't see anything, couldn't hear anything. Just the rustle of trees in the forest, and the crack and crackle of his rafters as the wind shifted them.

So, who the hell was at the door?

He opened it again, this time all the way.

"Hello?" he said, his voice cracking with tension.

No one there.

He stepped out onto the porch, and looked around.

Nothing.

Enough was enough, he decided. Whoever was playing this game, it was going to stop. Now.

Turning back inside, he grabbed his shotgun and his flashlight and headed for the door again.

Gun at the ready, he kicked open the heavy wooden door and marched out, swinging the powerful light around in an arc.

There was no one there.

He frowned, and looked around. He saw nothing.

But then, in the trees a few yards away, he noticed movement. Was someone standing out there? Straining his eyes, he picked up something pale and indistinct in the flashlight beam, moving in the breeze, as if he was glimpsing a shirt or a jacket belonging to someone who was waiting.

He peered at it.

This was some kind of stupidity, for sure. But he was going to investigate it. He had a shotgun, a flashlight, and a temper. Nobody tried to fool around like this with him, no matter what their motives were. He didn't put up with intruders. People must keep their distance from him, and would learn that lesson the hard way.

Angry, filled with intent, he marched across the clumpy snow, and into the forest.

But he'd only taken one step before he felt his foot catch against something, strung tight and hard near the ground.

A wire, he thought in surprise.

A tripwire, his mind told him frantically, as he heard a crashing, cracking noise coming from the tree above.

He should get out the way. That thing was coming down.

But the wire was looped around his ankle, and as he tried to move, he sprawled down, landing hard on his side.

A moment later, Ben felt a massive weight slam down from above, landing on his back, crushing him into the dirt.

87

The tree, he thought.

A huge branch had fallen on him.

The air was knocked out of him, and he sprawled on the ground, the tree landing on top of him, branches scratching, leaves and twigs cutting, the weight of the thing pinning him to the floor.

How had this happened? Had someone set this up?

Confused, he tried to piece together exactly how he'd ended up on the forest floor, trapped by a fallen tree.

"Help," he cried, but his voice was faint, a thread. The air had been driven out of his lungs and he couldn't get it back in again.

He tried to turn, to grope for his shotgun, but it was impossible. He couldn't move. He gasped for air. In panic, he realized the life was being crushed out of him.

"Help!" he breathed again, trying to twist away, trying to lift the tree off him. But it was too heavy, too big, and he didn't have the strength.

Ben lay beneath it, pinned to the ground, unable to move, his face pressed into the dirt, the breath driven out of him.

The ground was shaking.

And then he heard another massive cracking noise. Another branch was coming down on him.

He tried in vain to twist out of the way, but he was trapped and the branch was plummeting toward him, and he could only wait helplessly as it rushed down into his world.

He tried to scream, but the air had gone from his lungs and there was no breath in his body.

He heard the noise of the branch rushing through the air, and then a shattering crack.

And then, nothing more.

CHAPTER TWENTY

Wolfe pushed open the cabin's heavy wooden door, which had blown shut in the wind.

The wind had been his friend. The elements had been working with him. He'd been able to prepare his trap, using the tree branch, sawing at the wood, without the inhabitant of the cabin being aware.

He felt calmer now, as if he'd gained confidence in himself after a setback. He felt as if he could claw back the ground he'd lost.

Everything had worked exactly according to plan. The cabin was exactly what he'd expected. He breathed in wood smoke as he stepped inside.

It looked like something from the 1800s, he thought, closing the door behind him. Like a lumberjack's cabin or a trapper's shack. Dark wooden beams and a small fire. The coals were glowing, and the room was dimly illuminated by their light. He walked into the center of the room, his boots clumping on the wooden floor.

Beyond the main room, with its worn armchair, desk, and single bed, was a door. He hoped that, in here, he would find what he needed.

Wolfe pushed open the door to the bathroom.

A shower stood in the far corner and there was a basic toilet on the side. A bucket on a wooden shelf provided a makeshift sink. The wooden boards of the floor were cold and the air was damp. The room was lit by a small gas lamp.

On the shelf, he saw what he needed.

A pair of scissors and a razor that looked old, but still serviceable.

Quickly, Wolfe set about his work, doing what he needed to do. It wasn't what he wanted, but it was necessary for his survival.

He hacked at his hair and beard, tugging at the coarse strands, slicing the scissors through. Chunks of hair fell to the floor. He felt only the briefest regret as the cover that was his warmth, his camouflage, was cut away.

He soaped his face and carefully, using the razor, shaved his beard completely clean. His skin looked shockingly pale in the speckled glass of the mirror.

He worked carefully through his hair. He had enough skill with tools to be able to manage the scissors, even though the act of cutting his hair felt unfamiliar and strange. Although he was in a hurry, he needed his hair to look neat, a good job. Not a rushed task that might attract attention.

He methodically snipped the hair short, trimming it around his ears, as he'd seen in a book on army haircuts.

He took one last look, surveyed his work and nodded in satisfaction, running a hand over his newly shorn head. It felt cold and unfamiliar. His eyes looked wide and vulnerable. His thick neck looked pale, untouched by the sun. But he looked completely different.

He looked like an office worker who'd headed out into the wilderness for a vacation, Wolfe thought, with a flicker of surprise. Respectable. Not an outdoorsman.

He'd done what he needed to do. He was as good as new, ready to move on to the next stage of his plan. Returning to the main room, he shrugged the heavy furs off his shoulders and took off his leather jacket.

The wind rattled the window glass, and this time, it made him jump. Already, the temporary sense of peace he'd had was evaporating. It never lasted long. The feeling of threat was returning, and that was good.

If he became careless, they would get him. He needed that creeping sense of fear to keep him wide awake and on the alert.

He looked through the small rail of clothing, glad to find an outdoors coat there. When the man blundered outside earlier, into his trap, he hadn't put on a coat. Just as well, because even with his skill and ingenuity, Wolfe would not have found it possible to pull that heavy tree off of the man. It was crushing him, its thick branches also concealing him from view. Unless you knew he was there, you'd think it was just a massive deadfall. Or windfall. It looked natural. Hopefully, nobody would see him there for days.

He looked at himself in the mirror again, and turned around, studying himself from all angles.

The coat was a little tight on the shoulders, but otherwise, the new clothes were a good fit. That was a stroke of luck.

The coat was dark green and brown, good colors that would blend in with the outdoors. And waterproof. He might need that, in this weather.

Wolfe thrust his hands into the pockets, hoping to find the object that he was sure would be there, because it was the logical place to find it.

His fingers closed around a leather keyring.

Exactly what he needed.

There was no time to waste. Urgency flared inside him again. He'd already been here too long. They could easily have closed in on him. For all he knew, this man had a tracking device on his cellphone. If he dropped it and it broke, the object could send out a signal, and they'd be on him. He hadn't thought of that and had no idea if he'd had his phone with him or not.

What had he been thinking? He'd been arrogant, to think that he could come here, to this cabin, and hide his tracks so easily. He should have realized that they might already be on his trail, searching for him, scanning for him.

In this wind, could a drone fly? He glanced nervously at the window, hoping not, but wondering if unseen eyes were observing him.

Forcing himself to move, because fear had frozen him in his tracks, he gripped the keyring tightly. He'd been careless and if they had already figured out his location, then he might have already lost the game.

He turned and hurried out of the house, slamming the door behind him. He barely glanced back at the body under the tree. Already, it meant nothing to him. The man had played his part. He'd given Wolfe what he needed.

Now, he must move on.

It was time for the next stage of his plan. He walked outside, his breath clouding in front of him.

The sky was pitch black and the wind was howling with such force the cabin shook. It was going to be cold tonight. But that was good. The cold and the wind would keep people away. In his experience, it did.

He headed around the cabin, feeling sure that he was leaving footprints in the snow but there was nothing he could do about that. Hopefully, the wind would conceal them.

The key felt solid and reassuring in his hand.

He hurried to the lean-to at the back where the old gray pickup was parked.

It was unlocked. He climbed in and started it up.

Wolfe threw it in reverse and then hit the accelerator, swinging the pickup around. He was going to waste no time getting away from the cabin. He wanted to put as much distance between himself and it as possible.

He sped out of the cabin and took the road heading north.

Snow sprayed up from its wheels and the icy road ahead looked like a white ribbon. He pressed the gas pedal down further and the truck flew forward, heading away from the woods. Deciding to do the first leg of the journey on the back roads, Wolfe hoped he would avoid any roadblocks. He'd take the highway later, and then drive through the night, as fast as he could.

The wind was getting stronger. He could feel it tugging at the car. He could feel the cold, like icy fingers, reaching inside the vehicle. The heater didn't work well. But that was okay.

He was used to the cold. It was a familiar part of his life. With his coat, he would be warm enough, for now.

As he drove, he watched his mirrors carefully, staying vigilant for any signs of headlights behind him.

He had a lot of ground to cover tonight, and hoped to leave his pursuers well behind as he moved on to the next stage of his plan.

CHAPTER TWENTY ONE

Katie sat up in bed, gulping in air. She'd awakened from a nightmare that had been horribly real. She'd been pleading with Everton to tell her Josie's whereabouts. But he'd been laughing at her from the solitary cell.

And somewhere, deep in the night, she'd heard Josie screaming.

Her skin was prickled with goose bumps. Her nightmares were always worse when she was on a case and chasing down a killer.

The dream had been so vivid that she could still hear Josie's cries echoing in her ears.

Katie shivered, and rubbed her hands up and down her arms, trying to get warm. The room wasn't cold. It was a comfortable temperature. It was thanks to her nightmare that she was chilled to the bone.

At least the window was no longer fully dark. A pale shadow of gray filtered in. She checked the time.

Six-thirty a.m.

No phone call from Scott. That meant the killer had either not struck again, or else if he had, his kill had not yet been discovered.

It chilled her to think like this, but it was a necessary part of their reality.

In another half-hour, it would be light enough to get moving. It was time to start planning how she could get ahead of Wolfe, and predict where he would be.

She climbed out of bed, pulled on her clothes, and padded over to her computer.

It already had her case notes up on the screen. She pulled up the area map, and began filling in the information.

He'd started out in Colorado. Then he had stolen the car, fled to the border. Crossed on foot and made notably good progress north, to the place he'd set his trap.

And it was no surprise to Katie to see that he'd driven the stolen snowmobile still further north.

Katie leaned forward, and stared at the screen, unblinking.

Where will you be next, Wolfe?

She looked at the map, then at her notes, and then back at the map again. It was possible to make some educated guesses, based on the information she had. When she'd finished, she leaned back and studied the map again.

She felt strongly that he was heading into the icy northern wilds, racing away from civilization. The line on the map wavered slightly to the east and west, but it was overwhelmingly northerly. He might end up on the 97 highway, she guessed, but she didn't know how far he would go. It all depended on the end point he was trying to reach.

But this was assuming he obtained a car or a ride.

If he headed out into the wilds on foot or snowmobile, then he might follow the back roads and tracks, staying off any main roads at all. In that case, he could end up veering further east.

As yet, it was impossible to predict what he would do. She needed to take a better guess at his motives.

He might have a destination in mind. He could be heading for a lake, or a river that he knew about.

Or was he rushing to a person? The thought chilled her, but she had to consider it. He could be trying to track down a target. To add to his list of victims. So far, to her knowledge, he'd killed strangers. But that didn't mean he wouldn't move on to someone he knew.

She pulled on her jacket and boots, then tied her hair back into a ponytail. She took her gun, and checked the clip. She slid it back into her pocket.

Then she left her room. It was almost time to meet Leblanc and get going.

She walked downstairs, wondering if he would be waiting in the lobby.

He wasn't there, but she saw him outside, striding to the car with two coffees in his hand. He must have gotten them from the eatery next door.

She hurried through the bitter morning, feeling the cold filtering through her coat. Her boots crunched in the snow, sounding loud in the silence as she headed to the car. Leblanc opened the doors and they climbed inside.

The aroma of coffee filled the space. It smelled hot, rich and strong. Since she hadn't gotten much sleep last night, she could sure use a stimulant.

"Thanks," she said, with a small smile. No matter what the day would bring, it had started out well. The coffee was delicious. She took a long sip.

The sky was gradually growing lighter. A few snowflakes were whirling down, but the worst of last night's wind seemed to have abated.

The heater was blasting hot air into the front seats, slowly clearing away the fog. As it receded, Katie felt her senses sharpen. Taking a deep breath, she looked out the windshield, at the empty road.

They had a hard day ahead of them and she had no idea what it would bring, or how easy it would be to work together. She hoped Leblanc was going to maintain the better mood he seemed to have achieved. Was the coffee a sign of that, she wondered suddenly.

At that moment, he cleared his throat.

"I'm sorry about last night," he said.

Katie glanced at him, surprised.

"What do you mean?"

"I shouldn't have let my anger get the better of me. I was frustrated, in pain, feeling discouraged. But I shouldn't have made it your problem. It wasn't helpful. Your decision was correct. I knew that when you explained it. It would have been nice of me to agree."

Katie exhaled, and looked out the windshield. She wasn't sure what to say. She'd expected him to yell at her again, not apologize.

"So, I'm sorry," he said, quietly. "The painkillers kicked in. I slept well. I'm not going to let it happen again. Not today, anyway," he added wryly.

She found herself smiling. "Thank you," she said. "I appreciate what you've told me. And also that you think it was the correct decision."

It wasn't much of a response, but it meant a lot to her that he'd said what he had. Especially now, when her body and her mind were both feeling the strain of the case.

They didn't speak for a moment.

"It's frustrating that we still don't know what the killer's real identity is, or where he's headed," she said, returning the focus to where it needed to be. "I can see from the map he's going north, but I've no idea at what speed. I'm assuming he might have acquired a ride, or a vehicle. In which case, based on his trajectory so far, he might be hundreds of miles further north by now."

Leblanc nodded. "I was also checking the map this morning and thinking the same thing. But north is a big place. Where do we go? Where do we start?"

She shook her head. "I guess we can't get ahead of ourselves yet. First things first. We need to follow up where we left off, trying to see where he went last night, and helping the police check on the local residents. If we find a stolen vehicle, that'll be the most important lead."

She didn't want to think what might be found along with the stolen vehicle.

At that moment, the radio crackled.

"Winter? Leblanc?"

"Mills. What's up?" Katie listened, feeling tense, wondering if this incoming contact would prove to be good or bad news.

"I sent my teams out this morning, to check houses in the area. I've just had one of my officers get back to me."

"What did he say?" Katie felt a chill of apprehension.

"There's a guy who lives on the border of the woods, about two miles from where we lost Wolfe. Name's Ben Bouchard. My officers went around there this morning, and Bouchard is not there. The cabin's unlocked. His vehicle is missing and he wasn't answering his phone. They contacted me immediately. They're busy investigating further, but I thought I'd better call you. Do you want to go there?"

Katie exchanged a glance with Leblanc. This was right inside the zone where they had expected Wolfe to strike.

"Do we have the details on the car?"

"We're trying to obtain them. There's nothing registered in his name, so we're asking others who live close by if they knew what he drove."

"We'll head there straight away. Send the coordinates," she said. "We'll probably get there in ten minutes."

"I'll do that."

A moment later, the coordinates pinged into Katie's phone.

"This has to be him. It has to," Leblanc said.

Katie nodded. She put down her coffee mug and started the car, heading onto the main road and accelerating in the direction of the woods.

She had no doubt in her mind that this was Wolfe's doing. Fearing it was too late for Ben Bouchard, Katie could only wonder whether Wolfe had left them any clues as to where he'd gone.

96

CHAPTER TWENTY TWO

Ten minutes later, Leblanc peered anxiously out of the car window as Katie pulled up outside the isolated cabin. He felt tense and expectant about what they might find there. His heart accelerated as he saw an ambulance parked next to the police car. That didn't bode well.

The backdrop of tall, snow-capped trees made the humble wooden cabin seem even smaller by comparison.

As soon as he opened the door, the thrum of engines and the crackle of radios resonated through the still air.

The cabin door was open. Footprints crisscrossed the snow. Leblanc hoped that the officers would have taken note of any existing prints before marching up to the door, because now those tracks were destroyed.

He climbed out of the car, stumbling slightly as he did so. Although last night's rest had improved his injuries, he had painful bruises, and his muscles were stiff and sore.

"Where is everyone?" Katie muttered, hesitating as she strode over to the small house.

That was a good question, Leblanc realized. The door was open, but he could see nobody inside.

Looking at the trampled footsteps, he saw they headed around the cabin and into the woods. That was where he could hear the radios.

Feeling a sense of dread, he followed the tracks, and within a few strides, he saw the shocking sight.

A knot of people - police and paramedics - were clustered around a massive fallen branch.

Accepting the worst had happened, he hurried over.

One of the paramedics was kneeling by the body of a man that was only just visible, because it was crushed under what he now saw was two branches.

Leblanc hurried to the man's side.

"Leblanc and Winter from the special task force," he introduced them quickly.

"Morning. We arrived twenty minutes ago, and conducted a search. As soon as we walked around this way, we saw Ben Bouchard here.

Sadly deceased. Crushed by this tree," the man said grimly. "We can't fully assess him - have to wait for the branch to be removed - but we've cut some of the tree away to examine him. From what I can see, he's been dead a good few hours already."

Leblanc stared at the body. He could see the bloody scratches on Bouchard's face, and his sightless eyes. The massive log covered most of his chest and torso.

Had this been accidental? Leblanc doubted it, looking at the raw place on the stump where the tree had fallen. It looked cut.

Had he been lured this way and killed by Wolfe? All the evidence pointed to it.

Was there any other sign of a trap?

At that moment, looking down, he spotted the silvery wire around the man's foot, almost invisible among the fallen branches.

His senses tautened as he stared at it, imagining how the scene might have played out. Without a doubt, this was Wolfe's work.

"There's a wire here," he said, pointing to it carefully.

The paramedic looked at it and frowned.

"You think this was how he died?" he asked incredulously.

"It's thin, but it looks snap-locked around his ankle. You can see how it runs through the branches."

"Oh, hell. I don't believe this. Does it make any difference to how we handle the scene?" one of the paramedics asked, sounding shaken.

"It means you have to go carefully when you remove the branch. There might be more traps," Leblanc said. "This suspect is highly dangerous. Please proceed with extreme caution."

"Alright. We'll wait for more backup to get here before we proceed," the paramedic said, nodding somberly.

"Is there any update on Bouchard's vehicle?" Katie asked, turning to one of the RCMP officers.

The man nodded.

"He drove a gray pickup, according to a neighbor, who also remembered a couple of letters in the registration plate. We've done a search, and there's one in his father's name that looks to be the same. His father died a few years ago so we think Bouchard took over his vehicle. We've put an alert out for the vehicle, and the plates, already."

"Have you searched the house?"

"No, we haven't done a thorough search. As soon as we established he wasn't inside, we began looking further for him."

Leblanc glanced at Katie.

They headed toward the cabin's open door.

The house was semi-dark inside, and he could smell the musty scent of old wood, and perhaps a hint of mildew. The officers had placed foot covers at the door, and Leblanc put on a pair before walking cautiously in.

He was on high alert for any traps.

Katie was right behind him as he stepped through the small, simply furnished room.

The first thing he saw was a pile of discarded fur garments at the far end.

"Wolfe's clothing," he said softly. "That must belong to him. He must have changed."

"He could have set the trap for Bouchard, with the intention of getting inside and getting a change of clothes and a ride," Katie mused. "He knew you saw him. That might have motivated him to do this."

Leblanc didn't want to accept that terrible reality, but he knew he had to. The weight of responsibility was painful to bear. If he hadn't let Wolfe get away, Bouchard would be alive. Now, having been seen, Wolfe had done what he needed to in order to flee.

Guilt flooded through him, scorching and unwelcome. He pressed his lips together as he shouldered this burden.

Then he stepped into the small bathroom.

There seemed to be nothing unusual in the basic small room, and Leblanc was about to turn away.

But then Leblanc reminded himself to check and make sure, since they were up against a master of deception and concealment. He opened the trash can, and caught his breath as he saw the piles of dark hair that had been stuffed inside.

"He didn't just flee. He completely changed his appearance. He cut off his hair and beard," Leblanc concluded, feeling tense.

Without the hair and beard, would he recognize the man who'd attacked him? Leblanc doubted it. But Wolfe would find it easy to recognize him again. Now he had the advantage.

"Shaving hair, stealing clothes, stealing trucks," Katie said softly. She shook her head, looking at the items on the floor. "It's like he stole everything he needed to take on a completely new persona."

"I think this means he'll be doing his best to get as far away from here as possible," Leblanc said grimly.

Katie nodded.

"I agree. My guess is that he's been driving through the night. North, based on the route he's traveled so far."

"We need to urgently locate that pickup," Leblanc said.

They hurried back to the car and he got on the radio to officer Mills.

"The stolen pickup could be far out of the area by now. It's likely he's heading north. Please check all possible routes, and alert all roadblocks. He could easily be six hundred miles away, or more. And now, we're looking for a man with short hair. No long hair, probably a short beard, or no beard."

A moment later, he heard back from the station.

"We've issued an alert. We will check all of the major highways, and we're coordinating with the police in the towns going north."

"Good. Are there any highway cameras, or CCTV cameras at gas stations on that route?"

"We're going to put out an alert to them also," the officer assured him.

"If he's taken a pickup, he might have covered up the plates, or even stolen different ones," Leblanc said, remembering what a master of tactics Wolfe was. "Bear that in mind."

Had he done as much as he could to outthink this paranoid and violent man? Leblanc hoped so. They had severely underestimated this man's cunning, and now Ben Bouchard was dead. The suspect was driving around freely, while they were forced to play catch-up.

If only they could have gotten to Bouchard last night, they could have intercepted Wolfe before he made his escape.

It was a depressing thought, and one he quickly pushed out of his mind, telling himself it was impossible to predict where Wolfe would have gone.

"We can send the hair clippings in for forensic testing," Katie added. "Perhaps they might yield some clues to his identity."

"Good idea," Leblanc said.

He couldn't help feeling a sense of frustration that all of this was too little, too late.

But, at that moment, Katie's phone rang. It was Scott.

"We have a possible sighting," he said. "It's just been called in. In Merritt. A witness is reporting the theft of a motorcycle. Apparently it was stolen by a 'crazed mountain man' who set a crude trap."

"What kind of trap?" Leblanc asked, his mind immediately racing ahead.

"He strung a wire across the street. It knocked the rider off his bike. When he picked himself up, he saw the guy racing away on it."

Leblanc felt excitement surge, because this was definitely a similar *modus operandi*.

"Do you want to check it out? It's about an hour's drive from where you are now. I'll try and find more information shortly."

"We're on it," Katie said.

They turned and rushed to the car.

CHAPTER TWENTY THREE

Katie felt determined as she swung the car on the main road. Within an hour, they might have caught up with Wolfe, or else be speaking to a witness who would take them further in this complex case.

She gripped the steering wheel tightly as she acknowledged the pressure they were under. They had been so close to catching him yesterday, and yet he had escaped their grasp. It had not been Leblanc's fault. But they had underestimated what he would be capable of.

That lapse had cost a life. She would make sure that mistake was not repeated.

Katie had no doubt that Wolfe was highly intelligent. He had orchestrated a complex series of traps, and so far his plan was not showing any signs of failing.

Despite his intelligence, she was convinced they could catch him. His need to escape meant that he had taken risks, such as stealing a pickup and cutting his hair. He had taken those actions in order to achieve his goal, but they were still risks, and had yielded evidence. This evidence could be used to help track him, or even discover his identity.

They had come too close to losing him yesterday. She wasn't going to make the same mistake again. Her mind was working furiously, as she tried to anticipate Wolfe's next move. Switching vehicles would provide a break in the chain. She'd wondered last night if he might do that.

She glanced at Leblanc, who looked less sure as he frowned, taking in the deserted highway. The sun was low in the sky, angling through the scattered clouds, and the wind had picked up slightly.

"Are you sure he would have stolen a motorcycle?" he asked Katie doubtfully.

"It's the best lead we've had so far, and it's in the right direction," she replied.

She hoped that the eyewitness would be able to give them a detailed description of the thief, and that the description would point to Wolfe.

"Why is he headed north?" she asked aloud. "Is there anyone up there he knows? Someone who might hide him for a while? A familiar location he's seeking? There must be a reason."

"Maybe it's just the remoteness he wants," Leblanc suggested. "After all, he's clearly a survivalist. Also, he's a highly skilled hunter and tracker. He is a man who knows how to live off the land, and as we know, he's very good at improvised weapons."

"That's true," she admitted.

And we don't know what he looks like now, she thought with a shiver.

"Hopefully the eyewitness is able to describe him in detail." Leblanc was clearly thinking along the same lines. "If he does, we can assemble an identikit and circulate the pictures as widely as we can. We need to warn the communities, especially seeing as most are self-sufficient and don't interact much with the outside world."

Katie nodded grimly, thinking of how isolated those communities were. That would give Wolfe a huge advantage. It was not impossible that if he got far enough away, he might be able to disappear.

She floored the accelerator, driving as fast as she dared, aware that there were patches of ice on the road and doing her best to balance caution with speed.

Her phone rang again. It was Scott in communication with them.

"The local police have bagged up samples of the hair from Ben Bouchard's house, and are taking them straight to forensics. They're going to rush ahead with the DNA testing as fast as they can, and try to get back some preliminary results so we can at least see if it matches anything in the system. We're also going to take the discarded clothing and furs in, and analyze every item for any trace evidence."

"That sounds good," Katie said.

"We're continuing the hunt for the pickup. We've been notifying the gas stations and convenience stores along the main routes, and are asking them to check all of their cameras. So far, we haven't turned up anything, but we're pushing forward with the search. Every cop in the province is looking for that vehicle."

"Thank you," Katie said.

"Now, onto the motorbike theft," Scott said. "I agree there's a good chance he might have wanted to switch vehicles, and could have abandoned the pickup in the area. The witness reported the crime at the police station in Merritt. He's waiting for you there. So far, we have a description of the thief as being tall, wearing a brown jacket and gloves. We also have details on the direction in which he fled. So the local police are already taking on the search."

Katie glanced at Leblanc. That was sounding like it could be their suspect.

"We have the bike's number plate, and have circulated it within the wider area and to all traffic police."

"Was he armed?" she asked.

"Apparently not."

That, too, indicated it might be Wolfe, who had not yet used a gun in any of his crimes.

Katie hoped that this witness would be able to give them a highly detailed description of the thief, which would be enough for a sketch artist to work with.

*

Forty-five minutes later, Katie sped past the sign announcing the town limits. They were driving past the small, isolated houses on the outskirts of the town.

"We're close," Leblanc said, in a neutral voice.

And then, her phone rang once more.

"Listen up," Scott sounded excited. "We had another report just come in. There's been a sighting of the stolen pickup."

Katie gripped the wheel. This could be a game-changer.

"Where?" she asked.

"It was picked up on camera footage, just outside Prince George."

Katie frowned. "That's much further north, isn't it?"

"It's nearly three hundred miles further north. Too far to drive, given the urgency of this case, but I've organized a chopper that you can use if you want to follow that lead. The Merritt RCMP department has one ready whenever you need it. So it's up to you. Do you want to interview the motorcycle witness, or follow this new lead?"

Katie glanced at Leblanc. Two leads, two new chances to catch this elusive man.

She felt a rush of adrenaline. This morning, she had been worried that this trail might go cold, but they had been given two breaks in quick succession. She was determined to make the most of them. From the corner of her eyes, she saw Leblanc's jaw set.

"We need to make a fast call on this," she said. "If he gets away, we might not get another chance to catch him."

Leblanc nodded.

"We're going to need to move in both directions," he said. "Otherwise, I agree. He's outpacing us, and we're going to risk losing him."

"I agree. Let's tackle both leads simultaneously," she said, and saw him nod again.

"You head out in the chopper," Leblanc suggested. "I'll carry on into Merritt, and get the information on the motorbike rider."

Katie drummed her fingers on the steering wheel. She felt the thrum of excitement in her chest. Two chances. Two different routes to catching this killer.

"I'll put you through to the control room and they can organize the helicopter rendezvous," Scott said. "Good luck. I hope you find him – but remember to take care."

With a crackle, he disconnected.

CHAPTER TWENTY FOUR

Leblanc accelerated into Merritt, following the route to the police station. This town was a small hub where rivers and highways crossed, and he knew its population was around seven thousand.

That fact worried him slightly, because the sheer likelihood of a random motorbike theft occurring was going to be naturally higher in a town such as this.

He would have to focus carefully on the circumstances and description of this crime. He didn't want to chase after the wrong suspect.

There, ahead, was the police department, located squarely on the corner of the main street. Leblanc parked outside and climbed out. Immediately, the blast of icy air on his face reminded him that he was already further north.

Shivering, he marched into the station and headed straight to the front desk. Inside the building, he showed his badge to the desk sergeant.

"The witness is waiting for you," she told him. "His name is Rob Parks, and he's in the room at the end of the corridor, on the left."

"Thank you," Leblanc said. Needing to check, he asked, "Have there been any reports of an abandoned gray pickup this morning, or late last night?"

"No," she said. "We already sent a patrol vehicle through town to do a basic check, but we don't see any abandoned vehicles fitting that description."

Leblanc thanked her and headed in the direction she indicated.

As he walked down the corridor, he could see that this was a calm, organized place that hummed with a muted, purposeful activity. It reassured him. This was what the police did, and what he passionately believed in. Bringing order and justice to a chaotic and unfair world.

And yet, he had seen enough in his career to know that being a cop was not always so simple. Far from it.

He shook his head, trying to clear his thoughts, and knocked on the interview room door. He was here now, and there was nothing else to think about but catching Wolfe.

The interview room was small, neat and clean, and it felt very warm, almost airless, compared to the outside chill. The walls were bare and painted a uniform shade of pale blue.

There was the witness, waiting for him. He was in his early twenties and was sitting in a chair, his shoulders slumped in an attitude of defeat, and his hands resting on the desk. He looked up at Leblanc as he approached.

On the other side of the desk, a RCMP officer sat.

"Morning," the officer said. "I'm Detective Peterson, and this is Mr. Parks. I've interviewed him already and we have the word out. But we're still not sure if this thief is the suspect you're looking for, or not."

"Thanks for waiting, Detective Peterson. And for coming in, Mr. Parks," Leblanc said.

"I'm glad to help," the man said, his eyes showing the strain of the past hour. "Any chance of arresting that guy? I don't think I've ever been so shocked in my life."

"We're doing our best," Leblanc said with a sympathetic nod. "Can you give me a fuller description of the incident, and the thief?"

He sat down. This was a critical point in the investigation. He would have to assess whether this thief was likely to be Wolfe. A wrong call would mean a waste of resources and opportunity.

He couldn't let Wolfe slip away.

The man nodded.

"I was parked outside the shopping center on Main Street. I got on my bike and pulled off, and as I did, I saw this guy by the side of the road tug on something. The next moment I was riding into a wire. I tried to duck, but lost control of my bike and fell. He ran over and picked it up and rode off."

"How fast were you going?" Leblanc said sympathetically, wondering how much time this man would have had to notice the thief.

"Not fast. I mean, the fall was a shock, but luckily I wasn't hurt beyond a bumped knee."

"What do you remember about the man who took your bike?" Leblanc asked, keen to pick up any hints or clues. "How tall was he?"

"Probably six feet. He was a big guy, broad shouldered. He had a short, bushy beard."

Leblanc nodded.

Wolfe might not have shaved his beard completely. He could just have trimmed it. This could be their man.

"Which direction did he ride in?"

"He didn't head to the main road. He turned left, toward the outskirts of town," the witness said.

Detective Peterson spoke.

"The road that the thief took leads out of town, into an area of smallholdings and farms. We haven't had any notification of the bike being sighted rejoining a main road. We are short on staff, but we deployed two officers to search in the direction that the criminal took, and have set up a roadblock at the entrance to the main highway. If you like, we can head out and join the search."

Leblanc's interest was piqued. This could get them somewhere, and it would be a mistake not to follow up.

"Let's go," he said.

Leblanc followed the officer out, back into the cold.

They hurried toward one of the RCMP's patrol cars. As soon as they climbed inside, Peterson activated the radio.

"Where are you now?" he asked.

"We're working down Pine Lane."

"Okay. We'll head around the other side."

Activating the siren, Peterson sped away.

The car jolted and rumbled over a patch of potholes. Leblanc winced and tried to get his seatbelt better adjusted.

They drove down a narrow street at speed. Leblanc was surprised how small the town was. Already, they were on the outskirts, leading to an area of humble, tumbledown houses and cottages, set on large acreages.

"This is the poorer side of town," Peterson said. "The other side, to the south, is more sought-after. There are a few empty stands here, and abandoned farms. We have a pretty good picture of where they are, so that's where we're searching first."

He turned down a scruffy, muddy track.

The area was a patchwork of derelict land, with ancient trees and overgrown hedges. There were rusted, discarded farm machines and a few abandoned, boarded-up buildings.

Leblanc kept his gaze fixed on the light covering of snow ahead, looking for the distinctive tracks a motorbike would make.

"There," Leblanc said, urgently, pointing to an area of disturbed snow. "It looks like a bike track."

"You're right," the officer said, stopping and getting out. In the windblown snow, there were places where the tracks were clear and sharp. They veered to the left, into one of the abandoned-looking buildings.

Leblanc climbed out.

His heart was thumping with excitement. This was the break they needed.

"Let's check it out," he said.

The two officers approached the building. It was a timber structure, weathered and gray, with a sagging roof and broken windows. The door was open. The place looked abandoned, and the surrounding area was overgrown.

He could smell the sour stench of rotting wood and mold.

But it didn't sound abandoned. From inside, he could hear the sound of drills and the screech of metal.

He glanced at Detective Peterson and they both drew their guns. Then they moved forward.

Leblanc's eyes widened as he reached the door. Inside this dark, cave-like building, by the light of a few bright spotlights, a tall man, wearing a brown jacket and hard at work, seemed to be operating an illegal chop shop.

The floor was scattered with parts of cars and bikes. There were engines, wheels, and bodywork. Parts of different makes and models, all stripped down and ready for repair and customization.

In the center of the room he was busy stripping a motorbike, using a drill to take out parts.

He looked up, startled, as he heard them enter.

"Hands in the air! Now!" Peterson bellowed.

Leblanc noted his powerful build and short, bushy beard as he put his hands up slowly, looking horrified.

"Identify yourself," Peterson challenged.

But the man didn't. With a cry of rage, he threw a tool in Peterson's direction and rushed for the back door.

Peterson ducked as the tool flew toward him. It clanged against the wall behind him with a metallic thud. But Leblanc was already on the move, chasing after the man. No way was he going to escape.

Leblanc hurtled out of the back door, speeding after the fleeing thief.

He gritted his teeth. Despite his aches and pains, there was no way he was letting another suspect outrun him.

With a leap, he tackled the man. He got hold of his ankles and they both sprawled into the mud. The thief kicked and struggled but Leblanc hung on for grim death. He managed to grab the man's arm, and twisted it up behind him.

The thief let out a cry of pain. And then Petersen raced up with his weapon drawn.

"You are under arrest!" he yelled. "Get your hands behind you and cooperate with police!"

Leblanc wrestled the man to his feet and turned him roughly in Peterson's direction, quickly grabbing his handcuffs from his belt.

Once he'd cuffed the man, he finally felt it was safe to breathe again.

"Your name?" Peterson asked him again, angrily. This time, the thief replied.

"I - I'm Samuel Charles."

Peterson got on the radio and spoke rapidly.

Then he turned to Leblanc.

"Samuel Charles was arrested last week for suspected car theft, but he was released due to a lack of evidence. We can re-arrest him now," he said in satisfaction.

Leblanc didn't feel as pleased.

They had caught a criminal, but this man was not their killer, but rather a thief who had been operating in this area for a while. That meant he now needed to get north, as fast as possible, because more than likely, Katie was pursuing the correct lead.

Leblanc had to get to her as soon as he could.

CHAPTER TWENTY FIVE

Katie climbed out of the helicopter, shivering in the icy breeze, and hurried over to the passenger seat of the waiting police car. She'd never been to Prince George before. It was one of the area's biggest towns, a bustling center of business and industry. From the air, she'd been surprised by how large it was, especially for a place so far north.

"Agent Katie Winter," she introduced herself to the RCMP officer at the wheel.

"Officer Steele," he said, nodding. He was a sturdy-looking man with graying hair and a professional demeanor.

"How was the pickup spotted?" she asked, as they began driving.

"A gas station attendant, who'd listened to the police broadcast, thought he'd seen the vehicle in the early hours. He checked his camera footage and called it in. There's the gas station; we're passing it now. As you can see, it's on the way into town," Steele pointed.

"How clear was the footage?" Katie asked.

"Clear enough to see he was a tall man, green and brown jacket, big hood over his head. I've seen the visuals. That's as much as we have. We can't see his features."

"Has the car been seen leaving town at all?" she asked.

"The good news is no. We have been monitoring the highway cameras since then, and have set up a roadblock at the town's exit."

"Are there any other escape routes?" Katie wondered.

"There are some back roads, but so far there's been no sign of the pickup on them. We have gotten together a search party of police officers and a few civilians who are combing the area, but so far nothing's turned up."

"Does that mean that the vehicle has probably not left the area?"

"Exactly. We are monitoring the main roads and searching all the property that is accessible."

Katie's heart was racing. This was good news and bad. Good, because it meant the car was probably still here, but bad, because it meant that Wolfe could have abandoned it and decided to flee another way.

"Any reports of any stolen cars?" she asked.

"We've had no stolen vehicles at all reported yet."

They drove slowly through the town. It was late morning. The roads were fairly quiet. But the problem was that in a place this size, there would be no shortage of hiding places.

Where was the best place to hide a car? Where was the best place to pick up another ride, in such a small town, Katie wondered.

Think like Wolfe, she urged herself.

He would have been driving for hours. Tired. In a rush. He would have reached this town, probably, in the early hours of the morning and would have been able to operate under cover of darkness.

She thought the most likely reason for entering this town would be to get gas. He'd stopped at the gas station but he hadn't driven out. Not in that car. So perhaps he'd seen an opportunity. Or been looking out for one, and decided this was it.

He would have wanted to switch cars and get out. She felt certain of it. He would not be waiting around here, or hiding in town. Paranoid and fearful, he was at home in the wild, and would be feeling threatened and vulnerable in an urban area.

As her gaze fell on the signboard ahead, her mind kicked into gear and she realized what he might have done.

"That's a used car lot there?"

"Yes, it is."

"Let's go there," Katie said, urgently.

"You think he left the car there?" he asked.

"It's strategically located. Just a half-mile ahead after the gas station. If Wolfe had come here, he would have noticed it immediately. It doesn't seem to be well secured, and it looks like a logical place to leave a car, and get another one," she said.

Steele nodded and turned the car onto a side road. This led to the lot's entrance.

They parked the car and got out. A middle-aged man standing at the entrance to the tiny office saw them, and hurried over.

"Can I help you?" he asked.

"We're investigating a fleeing suspect, and wondered if he might have come past here. Have you checked this place, this morning?" Steele asked. "Do you know if any unfamiliar vehicles might be parked here?"

The man shook his head. "I've been collecting a car and just got back. My assistant opened up this morning but he did mention that the side gate was open. He thought I'd left it open last night. I remember

113

closing it up, but there was a bad windstorm, so I thought it could have blown open. We've never had a problem in the past, so we didn't think to check the stock. We have nearly fifty cars here."

Katie could see a range of cars, from battered four-wheel drives to high-end sports models that had seen better days. Heading to the back of the lot, she looked at the various plates and inspected the vehicles. She shook her head, walking around to the other side.

And then, her eyes narrowed as she saw a gray pickup, parked all the way at the end of the row.

Quickly, she checked the plates. They were a match.

Katie felt absolutely triumphant to have correctly followed Wolfe's thought processes.

"This is it!" she called. "He's left it here."

She hurried back to the owner.

"I need you to urgently check your stock. The suspect has left a stolen car here, and he's more than likely taken one of your vehicles. Can you see anything missing, at a glance?"

His eyes widened in surprise.

"Let me get my list," he said, and disappeared into the back office.

Katie's heart was racing. Wolfe had been and gone, under cover of darkness. He must have been rushing, pressured to leave before anyone noticed him there. Had he left something inside the pickup that could point the way to his whereabouts?

She hurried back into the lot, making her way to the pickup. Quickly, she approached the vehicle, her breath fogging up in the cold air.

She examined the truck, taking it slowly and carefully, looking for any possible sign of a trap. It had dirt on the tires, mud on the undercarriage, and two or three leaves stuck to the back window. She couldn't see any evidence of a trap. Knowing she would be opening the driver's door, Katie checked that out very carefully.

Then, she eased the handle open, and slowly pulled the door wide.

But, as she did so, she heard a strange noise. A scraping sound.

All her instincts flared. He'd managed to booby-trap the vehicle in a way that had escaped her careful check. She remembered the snowmobile with hideous clarity.

Even as Katie had the thought, she smelled the reek of gasoline.

She reached to slam the door again but she was too late.

With a whoosh, flames erupted.

But they didn't come from the pickup. They came from the car all the way at the end of the row.

And then, like a chain reaction, the fire spread, leaping from car to car. Coming toward her.

Katie recoiled in horror.

The flames shot upward, the smoke billowing, and Katie choked in terror as she flung herself away from the fire and into the next row of cars.

She landed heavily on the compacted dirt and rolled away.

Coughing, and gagging, Katie clambered to her feet and rushed away from the conflagration, gasping in horror as she saw the fire spread through the lot.

Behind her, a car exploded as the gas tank caught.

And then, another explosion.

She ducked as debris showered around her. Then, scrambling up again, she ran away from the lot, away from the fire that was spreading out of control. Another explosion split the air, and then another. The crackling of flames pursued her. Smoke boiled into the air.

Her mind was reeling as she took in the extent of the devastation that Wolfe had set up for her to trigger.

Katie reached the main road, where people were now running toward the scene. Officer Steele burst out of the office, together with the car salesman, who stared, horrified, at the destruction. Her breath burned in her lungs. Her hands were shaking.

"What happened?" the salesman asked incredulously, staring at the burning cars and then at her.

"It was the suspect. He set a trap," Katie gasped.

"Are you sure he isn't still here?" Steele asked.

"No. I didn't see anyone," Katie said, knowing that it was extremely unlikely that he'd waited around. This trap had been preplanned, the cars wired to explode when the pickup was opened.

This had been of a size and scale she'd never expected. Katie turned away, as the smoke in the air thickened. She'd only just gotten out in time. She could so easily have been trapped in that burning row of cars, or seriously injured in the subsequent explosions.

It was a terrifying thought.

And, by ensuring every car in the lot had gone up in smoke, Wolfe had effectively covered his tracks. They now had no idea what car he had stolen - if he'd taken any of them at all. It could even be misdirection, and he might have stolen another snowmobile.

Either way, he was hours ahead of them, free and clear.

Katie stared at the blazing cars. She couldn't help thinking that she should have been dead.

But she was alive. She was okay.

And she was even more determined to find Wolfe, and make him pay for what he had done.

CHAPTER TWENTY SIX

An hour later, with the fire under control and local police swarming the scene, Katie trudged back to the police vehicle that the RCMP had loaned her.

The thick, black smoke and the massive explosions had attracted a major crowd. She guessed that half the population of the town was gathered outside, cameras at the ready, talking worriedly among themselves as they captured the disastrous scene.

So many lives affected, she thought. So much property damage. And we didn't get him.

The thought made her stomach churn. But that wasn't the only concerning factor. It was more than that. It was the thought of what Wolfe might do next. He'd shown what he was capable of. A desperate man, fleeing law enforcement, might have yet more evil tricks up his sleeve as they battled to catch up.

Threading her way through the crowd, Katie arrived at the car.

She had wheels, but no clear destination to explore, and no idea where in the icy north Wolfe might be by now.

She climbed into the car and checked her phone.

There was a message from Leblanc, that he'd sent ten minutes ago.

"I organized a ride in a charter plane. I'll be there in thirty minutes. Can you pick me up from the airport?"

At least she had something to do, Katie thought morosely, starting the car and heading in the direction of the airport.

With a heavy heart, as she drove, she pulled out her phone and called Scott. She needed to brief her team leader on her failure, even though she could hardly bear to get out the words.

He answered on the first ring. "Katie. Where are you?"

"I'm on my way to the airport to meet Leblanc," Katie said, forcing herself to be calm and collected, even though she felt as if she'd made a terrible mistake, and could have done so much better if she'd thought ahead.

"I've been waiting for your call. I heard reports of a serious incident, something about a fire bomb at a car lot. What happened?" He sounded genuinely concerned.

"Wolfe escaped. He left the car he stole in a secondhand lot and set a trap. All the cars were set up to burn when I tried to open the door. It was a major destruction zone. At least ten cars were destroyed. They're still burning. Nobody can get close enough to identify which vehicles were damaged."

"I guess that allowed him to cover his tracks," Scott said.

"Yes. I should have predicted that, and shouldn't have opened the car," Katie said, feeling bitter regret.

"Nobody could have predicted that," Scott said sternly. "However, it is a setback."

"It means we've lost him, because we still don't know if he stole a vehicle, or which one it would have been. I've got wheels, but I don't know where to look for him," she said heavily.

"You think he's heading north?"

"Yes, that's what I thought earlier. He's been on a northern trajectory and I'm sure he will follow it."

"It seems he might be heading for a destination," Scott mused. "Not just fleeing randomly."

Katie sighed. "If we knew his identity, we might get a better idea of where. Was there any fingerprint evidence from the ID card he stole earlier?" she asked, wanting to explore every possible direction.

"No. Only the original owner's prints."

"And the DNA evidence from the hair clippings?"

"They're still working on that. It usually takes days, but they're going to try and get us some preliminary results sooner. I'm expecting those any minute."

"So we're back to square one? Is that what you're saying?"

"For now, yes."

Katie stared gloomily at the airport signage ahead.

She really didn't want to think about how her failure had impacted the team.

"I'm sorry," she muttered.

"Katie, I'm just grateful you are alive. You were lucky not to be trapped in the car when those explosions went off."

"I should have been more alert. I should have thought of it."

"Don't beat yourself up. You have a lot to do. Get to the airport, pick up Leblanc, and then you two strategize together," Scott's voice was stern now.

"I will," Katie said, with a deep breath. "I'm going to keep looking. I'm going to follow every single lead I can until I find him."

"Good. We'll be in touch soon," Scott cut the call.

The airport was ahead. On the runway, she could see a small plane landing. She pulled up in front of the building and got out.

The air was sharp, the clouds low and heavy with snow. She brooded as she waited, hoping Leblanc would reach her quickly.

In just a minute, he hurried out of the small airport, wrapping his dark jacket around himself in a theatrical way as the cold hit him. Even in her gloom, Katie couldn't suppress a flash of amusement at her partner's character.

He hurried to her, and she saw worry in his eyes. He looked stressed. She couldn't blame him.

"I just heard about the fire bomb. I can't believe it," he said, climbing into the car.

"I was careless. I could have been killed, and I allowed evidence to be destroyed. But he's more than likely hundreds of miles ahead of us, Leblanc. He keeps managing to cover his tracks and then it feels like we're starting from scratch every time. We can use this car if we need to; the Prince George police department has loaned it to us, but I have no idea where to go."

Katie started the engine and turned on the heat, appreciating the warmth as it blasted through the vents.

She could see the smoke from the used car lot still lingering in the air, but it was dissipating now. She guessed the crowds outside would be starting to leave and go about their day.

"Shall we get onto the road? Start driving? If only we knew where he was heading," Katie said in frustration.

"Well, I think we should follow our usual procedure," Leblanc said. "We need to go through everything carefully and see if we can narrow down the options. Let's start with the assumptions we can make."

Glad to have the benefit of his cool logic calming down her frustrated thoughts, Katie turned her mind to what they did know so far.

"We know that he is heading north and perhaps trying to get to a specific northern location. We don't know if he is heading for a certain destination, rather than just randomly fleeing."

"We know he's talented at thinking on his feet and that he's changed his appearance," Leblanc added. "And that he's desperate, and more than happy to use extreme violence if necessary."

"I don't think he can have made a lot of preparations in advance," Katie said. "I think we have to assume he's acting on the fly, making decisions as he goes. The problem is he's very good at it. He's extremely resourceful."

"Exactly," Leblanc nodded. "What about his identity? Anything new on that?"

Katie was about to say no, when her phone rang again.

It was Scott on the line.

"Scott?" she answered quickly. They'd spoken just a few minutes ago, so if he was calling back, it must mean he had new information, and that made her feel hopeful once again.

He sounded excited.

"We have a breakthrough at last. We got a DNA match from the hair clippings. They've done partial tests, on the new sample, but it's close enough to be sure. The suspect's last known residential address is a farm a few miles north of Hazelton. That's about a five hour drive from where you are now. I've checked, and it won't be easy to organize a helicopter at short notice from Fort Nelson. It will take another two hours, minimum, for one to be available. Given that, you might as well get on the road."

Katie exchanged an excited glance with Leblanc.

Finally, they had him!

"We're on our way," she said.

She pushed the gear lever into drive and floored it, heading out of the airport and turning toward the highway, heading north.

CHAPTER TWENTY SEVEN

Leblanc quickly fastened his seatbelt. Katie was driving like a demon, but he didn't care. At last, they had a solid lead. DNA evidence was something he'd never even dared to hope for.

Once they were on the road, he called Scott back while Katie focused on the wheel.

"This suspect has a record. That's why we were able to get a result so quickly," Scott told him.

"Who is he?" Leblanc asked.

"His name is Marius Roman," Scott replied. "He's a sixty-four-year-old man who has former convictions for assault and battery. He was last paroled fifteen years ago. There were a couple of earlier stretches in prison, too."

"Sixty-four?" Leblanc echoed in amazement. This man was much older than he'd thought. He'd fought Leblanc with the power and speed of a younger man. He was shocked to find he was so old.

"And his residential address?" Katie asked.

"It's a small farm. I'm going to get in touch with the local police, and brief them on the situation now. I'm of two minds about asking for backup. They're thinly stretched out there, and we're dealing with an exceptionally dangerous individual."

Scott's resigned tone acknowledged the vast distances and scarce resources they were dealing with.

"If they could organize a roadblock further up, that would work," Katie suggested.

"I'll do that," Scott promised.

Leblanc hung up, and he and Katie traded triumphant glances.

"We have him," Leblanc said, breathing a sigh of relief. He knew that it was premature and that there would still be a long journey to their killer.

But having a name. An identity. An address. Those were big wins. Suddenly the ghostly man they had been chasing had become a rock-solid, real criminal. With a record. With an address.

It meant everything to know who he was.

Leblanc stared ahead at the gray horizon, counting down the miles.

Four hours later, they drove through the tiny settlement of Hazelton, on the junction of the Buckley and Skeena rivers, which was located a few miles south of the farm. This village numbered only a couple of hundred inhabitants, and it was extremely remote.

The day had grown darker and now there was a chill in the air. The sky was a gray blanket, the color of stone, and snow was predicted to fall as evening closed in.

Leblanc's stomach felt tense. The area they were in felt impossibly deserted, and icy cold.

He felt uneasiness growing, gnawing at him. What would they find when they reached the farm? He was afraid that Marius would have disappeared from his house by the time they got there.

His phone rang. It was Scott, updating them on the situation.

"There's a highway junction about twenty miles on from the farm. Police are setting up a roadblock just before that junction. So, if he makes a run for it, he won't be able to get away. They'll also post officers on the lookout to the south, near Hazelton. I believe they're moving into place already. So if he's at home, he can't run for it."

"That's good," Leblanc replied. He felt tension coil inside him.

He cut the call and stared ahead expectantly.

"Here's the farm," Katie said.

This was it. They had reached the destination where their suspect lived. A broken-down gate, hanging open, marked the edge of Marius Roman's land.

The place looked isolated and wild, with pine trees scattered across the landscape and rolling hills that were covered in snow.

The long, winding track that led through the farm gate and onto Roman's land was unpaved and covered in potholes. Katie steered around them as the car bumped and jostled.

There was the farmhouse ahead. Leblanc's stomach tightened as he saw the building.

The farmhouse was in a state of disrepair. It was a dark wooden cabin with a steep roof. It looked old and lonely.

No one was outside, and the grounds around it were overgrown and wild. A derelict barn stood a little way away from the house.

"This place looks completely abandoned," Katie said in a low voice, edging the car forward. They were both scanning the track ahead anxiously and with care. There was a high likelihood that this man would have acted in character, and set traps for any law enforcement that might pursue him there.

It gave Leblanc a sick feeling to think what might happen if they missed one that was set up on this man's home turf.

The car bumped across a field, and they passed a small, rickety shed on the right.

Katie drew in a sharp breath, and Leblanc's heart accelerated as he saw what she'd seen.

A thread of smoke, coiling from the farmhouse's chimney.

"Marius is at home," Leblanc said, through tight lips. "Or someone is."

They stopped about fifty yards away from the farmhouse.

Even so, Leblanc knew that in this silence, this emptiness, there would be no way of arriving unannounced.

And he was right.

As they climbed out of the car, the house's front door opened. A tall, broad-shouldered man stood there. Aggression emanated from him as he placed his hands threateningly on the doorframe, blocking the way in with his large, solid body.

His hair looked thick and unruly, and the silver-gray locks had been roughly chopped with shears into a ragged, short style. He was cleanly shaven. Leblanc noticed this immediately, comparing it to his mental checklist of the killer.

Every fiber of his body felt on high alert as he paced carefully across the scrubby, snow-covered ground, looking around for any triggers or wires.

"Marius Roman?" Katie asked.

His face looked cold and hard. His lips were a grim, bloodless line. His hands were big, bunched in fists.

"That's me," he said, in a deep, throaty voice. "Who are you?" His eyes were alert and intelligent.

"Law enforcement," Katie replied briefly. "Mr. Roman, you are under arrest." Her voice was firm as she stepped forward, reaching into her jacket to take out her cuffs. "We've obtained DNA evidence linking you to recent serious crimes further south."

Roman said nothing. Leblanc's gaze sharpened, and he looked for any sign of aggression in his eyes.

There was none that he could see. But, as they stepped forward, that suddenly changed, as if a switch had been thrown.

"You're not bringing me in!" Marius shouted. His voice was powerful and loud. It was filled with rage.

"I didn't do anything," he roared. "You're not taking me in! DNA evidence? What fakery is this? I know my rights! You have no right to come onto my property and make a false arrest!"

Leblanc saw murderous fury blaze in his face. Then, with a roar, Marius lunged forward.

In a flash, his fist lashed out. The blow caught Katie in the right shoulder.

It caught her by complete surprise. She stumbled backward and fell, rolling away. Leblanc saw that she was groping for her gun, but after the vicious blow, her arm was numb.

Leblanc knew he had to contain this situation, and fast, because Marius was drawing his fist back, ready to drop him, too. No time to get his gun. Adrenaline surging, he flung himself forward and grabbed the big man's arm.

But Marius's other hand lashed out, and his fist caught Leblanc a blow in the neck.

It wasn't hard enough to crush his larynx, but it was painful and suffocating. Leblanc recoiled, choking.

He got his hands up, ready to mount a defense against the onslaught, but Marius's fist was already lashing out once more.

The blow hit him in the gut, and Leblanc felt his breath whoosh out. He doubled over, fighting for breath. Another blow caught him in the temple, and the world spun.

Marius was a furious, raging bull. But Leblanc was a trained officer.

Finally he got his balance, and got the measure of his attacker. He dodged the next onslaught, swaying back as a blow whistled by his ear. Then, his hands shot out and he grabbed Marius's shirt, pulling him forward. He was incredibly strong, but Leblanc got him off balance. Taking the opportunity, he punched him hard in the solar plexus, hearing a breathless grunt as his blow hit home.

Marius staggered back, then swiped out, catching Leblanc with a sharp blow to the head.

His neck snapped sideways and he stumbled back, feeling dizzy and disoriented.

In a moment, Marius was on him. He grabbed for Leblanc's throat, readying his fingers to crush it. Leblanc managed to grab his arm and

124

twist it backward, but Marius shoved him down so that his head bashed into the snowy ground and all his bruises screamed in protest.

He could kill him, Leblanc realized, battling to get his knee up for another offensive blow. He was that angry. The man was in a murderous rage. This situation had escalated all the way out of control, and in a frighteningly short time.

But then, finally, out of the corner of his eye, he saw Katie had managed to regroup. She'd gotten her gun out of the holster using her left hand, and pulled herself to her knees.

Then she stood, aiming the gun at him with her left hand rock-steady. Her face was icy cold, calm and contained.

"Enough!"

Her voice was sharp. Her gun was leveled at Marius's head. The man's gaze veered to her face, and he froze.

Katie aimed the gun at his head, her hand steady and firm. She didn't blink. For a moment, the only sound was their harsh breathing.

Slowly, reluctantly, Marius struggled to a kneeling position and raised his hands.

Leblanc's head was throbbing. Quickly, he got the handcuffs over the big man's wrists.

"You're going to jail, Mr. Roman. You're under arrest. This is over now. It's all over."

But Leblanc felt a flash of unease as they manhandled him inside the house, to wait for the police van to arrive. The look in his eyes told him that the other man still didn't think it was over.

Despite being cuffed and under arrest, he didn't think it was over at all.

CHAPTER TWENTY EIGHT

An hour later, it was fully dark, and Katie was ready to interrogate the suspect. They'd followed the police van to the closest RCMP detachment, which was in the village of New Hazelton. The village was nothing more than a couple of cross-streets, and the RCMP building contained a front desk, a back room, and one interview room, as well as a tiny jail cell.

"Are we ready?" she asked Leblanc in a low voice before they stepped inside.

"Yes. Let's go do this," he said determinedly.

Taking a deep breath, Katie walked inside to face the suspect. This was going to be a vitally important interrogation. Katie wanted this case to be rock solid. The DNA evidence was in their favor, but she knew that what Marius would say now would provide an essential part of the full picture. She wanted to get a confession from him. That was her goal.

The tall man was handcuffed to the metal desk. Now that they were in the harsh light of this tiny office, Katie noticed a thick scar running down his left cheek. His silver gray hair was thick and raggedly cut. His eyes were dark, cruel, and intelligent.

As she and Leblanc sat down opposite him, she found herself remembering that the suspect was the same man who had brutally killed a series of innocent people, and who had shown no remorse. The same man who had almost killed them both just now.

Now, they needed to make this case watertight.

There was a lot of ground to cover. For a start, they needed to find out how Marius had gotten back home. There was no sign of a stolen vehicle on his premises. Only his ancient pickup, held together by rust, parked in the shed.

However, Katie acknowledged that someone as cunning as their killer could easily have hidden a car so well it might never be found. There was certainly enough space to do so, in this massive, deeply forested, thinly populated part of the world.

She took a deep breath and forced herself to focus.

"Mr. Roman, we have questions for you."

He stared back at her with a defiant gleam in his eyes.

"Go ahead," he said.

"Did you leave your property in recent weeks? Did you travel out of the area or over the border? Have you recently returned?"

He shrugged. "No. I was on the farm. Where I always am."

"Can you account for your movements? Any proof you were there? Did anyone see you? Did you interact with anyone, make calls, drive anywhere?"

He shook his head.

"Answer this question. Did you leave the farm at any point in the past few weeks?"

He stared at her with an unwavering look. "No," he said firmly.

"I don't believe you," Katie countered.

Marius shrugged. "You're wasting your time. You might think I'm your man, but I'm not. I went nowhere. What crimes was I supposed to have committed?"

"A series of murders," Katie told him, her voice flat and cold. She wasn't going to reveal further details. He knew full well what he'd done. "The DNA evidence from hair left at one of the scenes links you to it. We'll take further samples from you just now to complete the chain of evidence."

He sneered at her. "You can take what you like. I didn't do what you think I did. I'm innocent, and when I have a lawyer, I'll be walking out of here."

Katie felt a flash of anger. "Don't be so sure about that. You just assaulted two police officers. That's a serious offense, right there on its own."

Marius's face darkened, and he bunched his fists. Katie saw his knuckles were bruised and swollen.

"That was self-defense. Nothing more."

His eyes met hers defiantly. She saw already that he knew he would lose that argument in court. But yet, he wasn't capitulating and telling the truth.

She hated the feeling of uncertainty that was creeping through her. There was no reason to be anything but confident when facing up to this strong suspect.

Or was there a reason for her own doubt? Was she missing something?

Katie suddenly started to wonder why she was second-guessing herself. Could she be picking up on subliminal evidence? If so, she'd better start listening to what her instincts were telling her.

"Did you drive your truck out at all?" Leblanc asked Marius again.

"No."

"Did anyone from the village see you in the past few days?"

"No one from the village ever sees me, except to get supplies from the store. And that's only about twice a year. I hunt. I fish. I don't go there, and they don't come here."

"Do you trap?" Leblanc asked.

Katie hoped this question might crack through Marius's defenses, but he remained impassive.

She could see Leblanc didn't believe Marius and was convinced of his guilt.

It was only Katie who was becoming less sure.

Drilling down into the reasons for her own uncertainty, Katie realized it was nothing to do with what this suspect said. It was how he looked.

For some reason, something about his appearance was ringing alarm bells in her mind.

"If you're not ready to say anything more, we'll let you sit alone for a while," Leblanc said.

He stood up and left the room. Katie followed him. Outside, he closed the door carefully and then shook his head.

"Denying, all the way down the line. With nothing. No alibi. No interaction with anybody. I think this denial adds to his guilt. It's not going to be a problem. The way he attacked us, combined with the DNA evidence, and his criminal record, I don't think a jury would hesitate in a guilty verdict." Leblanc sounded satisfied. "We're wasting our time asking him anything. Let's just move ahead with the charges."

One of the RCMP officers who had been listening through the glassed window, hurried into the corridor.

"I agree. If he won't talk, there's no point in questioning further. Let's process his arrest, and I'll call for transport to take him to the district's main prison."

But Katie shook her head. Now, as she thought some more, doubt was filling her.

"Can you wait a minute?" she asked.

"Why?" Leblanc asked, incredulously.

"Just give me a moment."

"What do you want to do?"

"I want to ask him a few more questions. I feel sure we're missing something," she said, wishing she could pinpoint what was bothering her so badly.

Leblanc's eyes widened. "This is a waste of time. He's guilty, and he's dangerous. We can't hold him indefinitely. I've seen the message from Scott. He's convinced that the evidence is more than sufficient. He wants us to close this, and head home."

Katie bit her lip. She wanted him to be guilty. Perhaps she was wrong, she thought. Perhaps she should just accept that he was guilty, and the case was closed.

But Leblanc's own words were making her even more resolute to explore her misgivings.

"He'll kill again."

If they had the wrong man in custody, that would happen. And, suddenly, Katie realized exactly what was troubling her.

As soon as you saw it, it was as clear as day. Confidence filled her again. She had been correct. There was more to be asked.

"Trust me," she said to Leblanc. Before he could answer her, she turned and walked back into the small room.

Marius looked up at her, his expression angry, challenging.

She took a deep breath.

"I don't think you killed anyone," Katie said.

He glared at her for a second. "That's not what you said a moment ago," he countered. "I'm not falling for your tricks. I know how you play people."

Katie stared at him.

The highlights in his steel-gray hair shimmered under the lights.

It was his hair that had finally made Katie realize what she'd missed. What they'd all missed.

Gray hair. Darker gray, but she remembered the chopped tufts of hair and beard that they had found in the cabin's trash can. Those had been closer to black. Uncompromisingly dark. Yes, the room had been gloomy, but in the glare of the flashlight, she had noticed only a few threads of gray.

She realized that there must be a substantial age difference between the man in this chair, and the man who had cut his hair and fled under cover of night.

And yet, the preliminary DNA, that had led all of them in the wrong direction, was matching up.

Therefore, it was time to ask the question she needed to. The question that might crack this case once and for all and lead them to the real killer.

"Mr. Roman, do you have a son?"

He stared at her with a look so hard, it could have been carved in stone.

"Yes," he said. "I have a son."

Katie let out a deep breath, feeling the excruciating tension in her shoulders ease just a little. Now, she was sure she was on the way to the truth.

"When was the last time you saw him?"

He shrugged. "Not for years. Not for decades. We didn't get along."

"Do you know where he lives?"

He shook his head. "He left home long ago."

"Where was home?" Katie knew this was a pivotal question. "Was home where you live now?"

"Why do you want to know this?" Marius's eyes were narrowed as he stared at her.

"I think your son is the killer."

He pressed his lips together.

"Where did you live, when he was younger?"

"Why should I tell you this? Why should I tell you anything? You're police. Scum. You're not going to let me go!" Marius spat.

"We're not going to let you go until we've caught the real killer. You're going to stay here in the jail, until we do. But if you help us catch the right man, we will drop the charges of assault that we've opened against you. That's a promise, and this interview is being recorded. So you have proof of it."

She took another deep breath.

"We're going to work together. I need you to tell me everything you know. Where you lived. What you remember about your son. What he did, and where he went, when he left home."

He was glaring at her, as if he wanted to kill her. He didn't speak.

She stared back impassively, taking this all the way down to the wire.

"We can do this the easy way, or we can do it the hard way. It's up to you. Do you want to stay in jail for the rest of your life? Do you want to rot in jail, knowing that the real killer is out there, killing innocent people, because you're protecting him?"

Marius finally capitulated. His shoulders slumped.

"I have no reason to protect my son," he muttered.

"Then tell me what I need," Katie said. "Starting with his name."

"His name is Brock," Marius admitted.

"Where did you live?"

"We lived further north," Marius said. "Up near the Yukon border. We ran a fur business. Trapping, shooting. We sold pelts. Mostly to export companies. It was profitable for a while, but then Brock wanted out. He left."

His voice was bitter.

"Why did he leave?"

"He didn't want to be a part of the business. He didn't care about it."

"Did he have any training in trapping?"

"Yes."

"Was he good at it?"

Roman nodded. "He had the magic touch. A real instinct for how to catch animals. I taught him everything I knew. He was so good; he was better than me. He was better than anybody."

Katie nodded.

"He should have become the master. He should have been happy, running the business. But he left, and then I moved away."

"We are trying to trace him. He's fleeing north."

Roman considered this.

"He might be looking to go back to our old place. To our old hunting ground. It's close to the Yukon border, about twenty miles north of a ghost town called Centreville. He knows that area well. He knows every tree, every rock, every crevice. We have a house there. If he's fleeing, I would guess he'll go there."

Roman leaned forward and spoke in a low voice.

"One thing I should tell you. My son is dangerous. I've known that for years. Ever since he was a teenager. He's not right in the head. He's paranoid. He believes people are after him."

"What are you saying?" Katie asked, feeling coldness fill her.

"He won't be looking to hide away. He'll be looking to fight back. If you go there, and follow him, I am sure that he will try to destroy you," Roman said, in a low, harsh voice.

Katie nodded. "Thank you," she said.

She left the room.

"We need to get going as soon as possible," she said quietly to Leblanc. "The more time we take to get there, the more time it will give him to prepare."

CHAPTER TWENTY NINE

At last, he had come full circle. It had been years, Wolfe thought, as he pulled up outside the wooden cabin where he'd grown up.

He was back in the territory of his past. For a moment, his real name flitted through his memory. Brock. That was what he had been called, when he'd been under his father's rule.

His dad had been a bully. Domineering. He'd forced Brock to obey him. And he'd had a sixth sense about him, too. He'd watched him the whole time. Brock had always felt his father's eyes were on him, knowing his movements, even guessing his thoughts.

From the time he'd been young, he'd been a marked man, he realized. Targeted.

He had left his name behind, hoping anonymity would allow him to make his escape. He had chosen Wolfe. That was who he was now.

He climbed out of the stolen car, a relatively new Land Rover that had eaten up the miles, fast and powerful. It had been an endless, exhausting drive, but Wolfe had never needed much sleep, and now there were things to do.

In this area, he knew he could make his stand. He could destroy whoever came after him. And then, he could disappear. He knew exactly how to do it and where he could go.

He would spend the rest of his life doing what he needed to. Trapping. Building his defenses. And then, launching attacks to keep his territory safe.

Anyone who strayed nearby would not live to get away. He would make sure of that, and he would remain hidden.

The cabin was cold. He hadn't been back here in years, and he'd left it closed up.

Wolfe had never worried too much about heat. He was born hot. His blood was fiery.

He opened the door and memories surged back.

Good and bad. The good memories of finding prey struggling in his trap, knowing that he'd succeeded in outwitting them with his cunning and skills. Memories of heading out alone, knowing he could withstand the ice and cold, that he was moving unseen within the harsh landscape.

The bad memories of his father's anger. Of being brutally beaten, denied food, locked inside. A very early memory of his mother leaving. He'd barely known her at all and could not remember what she looked like.

Pushing those thoughts aside, Wolfe walked in and looked around. The place was exactly as he'd left it, years before. Of course, nobody had come here. It was too far from anywhere. Tucked away in a rugged, mountainous area, it was home only to the wild animals that roamed.

There was a single bedroom, with a bathroom, and a kitchen with an old stove. Wolfe had slept in the kitchen, bundled up on furs.

He'd spent many winters here, and knew every inch of the forest and mountains, for miles and miles. There was a creek running behind the house, which snaked through the valley. There were cliffs and gullies and deep, forested areas where he'd learned to track the most wily, dangerous prey.

It was his territory. But he knew they wouldn't think so. They would want to take it. And capture him.

Into his mind swam a picture of the man he'd fought with. Dark hair, dark eyes. An intense expression.

He felt a deep, simmering anger. He knew that the man would come after him. He felt sure.

He would come, and Wolfe would destroy him.

Most likely, they had found a way to track him, despite the precautions he'd taken. Wolfe was wary of their powers and knew that he should hope for the best, but plan for the worst. The worst-case scenario was that the man would be here soon. Probably, he would bring backup with him. Wolfe was not sure how many would arrive but he was sure they would swarm here, in their numbers.

They wouldn't be able to surprise him. Wolfe had eyes all over, and he knew how to use them.

The man had a weapon, but Wolfe did not fear weapons. To use a weapon, you had to be able to see your target, and Wolfe did not plan on being seen.

Not until his targets were no longer a threat.

They would want to kill him, but he would be ready for them. He would outsmart them. He'd prepare for them, neutralize them, and then he would disappear.

Others might be able to find him. Perhaps. But he would be ready for them, too.

He felt as if years of planning had gone into this moment. Soon, it would be time to begin. He'd have to follow his instincts. It was all down to instinct, now.

But first, he needed to rest. He'd gone too long without it and would need his strength.

He lay down on the pile of furs, so old and dusty. He didn't care. Sleep came quickly and wrapped him in blackness.

*

An hour later, he was up, wide awake, and prowling the woods. His head was full of plans.

He walked across the frozen creek, and headed along its bank, trying to strategize what he could do in order to outsmart them. There were many factors, and he could expect many unknowns. He had to make up plans in advance, but be ready to change them.

He had to prepare for any eventuality. And be alert.

Wolfe's eyes were sharp. He'd always been gifted with exceptional vision, even in the dark.

Most likely, they would approach from the front. If they arrived in a helicopter, there was only one obvious landing point. That was the clearing in the valley. So he could predict that they would land there, and the noise would alert him.

It was the perfect spot for an ambush. He walked through the tree line, and then down the hill, playing out scenarios in his mind. It was familiar to him. In this area, he had run, played, hunted. He'd been soaked by storms and frozen by snow. He knew every inch by heart.

He planned to use the terrain to his advantage. One trap would not be enough. He needed many.

Think of every eventuality, he reminded himself. Don't assume you know how they will attack.

The wind was pulling at his clothes, and whipping his hair. It was cold, but for him, the cold did not matter.

This was where his first trap would be, he decided. They would land the helicopter and enter the woods, following their target. They would be looking for Wolfe. But he would not be there. He was already prepared.

Then, he could set traps along the valley, and at the creek. He could hide and wait.

He would make sure to remain invisible. They would blunder into his traps, no matter how careful they thought they would be. That was Wolfe's talent. He knew where people would go and how they would think.

Once they were incapacitated, he would kill them. But before he killed them, he would make them wish they were dead. He'd learned from his previous mistakes. Killing alone was not enough. He needed to leave examples behind him, to scare off others who might try and follow him in the future.

He would make them suffer. He would take out his rage at all of them, those who had hunted him, who had hounded him, who had wanted to take everything that he had.

They had tried to strip everything from him. His freedom. His safety. They had been watching him, day and night. It was time for retribution now for everything he had suffered. This was going to be payback.

He got down off the outcrop, and then walked carefully back to the house.

His scheme was clear in his mind. It was time to get to work.

He needed to make sure his hunters got the welcome they deserved.

CHAPTER THIRTY

Katie watched the road scroll by in silence, the car's headlights splitting the night. It was a long drive. They'd been behind the wheel for eight hours. She and Leblanc had taken turns at driving, while the other tried to get some rest.

They had discussed using a helicopter and what the advantages would be of speed over stealth. It would have gotten them there faster, but in the pitch dark, landing would have been more dangerous and also Wolfe would know when they arrived. In the dark, traps would be more difficult to see. They were up against a lethal adversary, and could not afford to give him any advantage.

They'd discussed involving others, but they had both agreed that more manpower simply meant more risk.

So, it was the two of them against him. They were hoping that by taking a route through the back of the farm, they could surprise him.

They'd stopped once for gas and fast food, at a remote pit stop in a town that comprised no more than a few scattered lights.

The ghost town they'd passed earlier, Centreville, had been invisible – no more than the skeleton of a long-abandoned mine trading center. They'd also passed Jade City, which was nothing more than a point on the map signaling the area that was rich in serpentinite, greenstone, and Nephrite jade.

Katie was sure that Wolfe had made the same stop, followed the same route.

They were almost at their destination. And it was almost dawn.

There was a dim light on the eastern horizon, and the coordinates of Wolfe's childhood home were just a few miles ahead.

The road was narrow and winding, and it was hard to see in the predawn gloom. Leblanc was at the wheel, and driving very carefully. Katie feared with a cold certainty that they were already observed, even though they had switched the headlights off.

"Hold on," she said. "The back route starts here."

Leblanc turned into the dirt road that would take them down the hill and through the trees to the valley.

They needed to surprise him.

She felt sure he would be waiting for them to attack, guns blazing. Using a helicopter, or a convoy of vehicles. That was what he would expect.

Not two people, sneaking in from an unexpected direction.

Leblanc found a small gap in the thick stand of trees, parked there, and climbed out.

The air felt harsh and icy. She could smell fresh snow and the faint scent of pine.

Now, they needed to close in on foot, quickly and quietly.

Katie took a deep breath, and then eased forward along the faint track. She could hear an owl calling, and the wind sighing through the branches, but there were no other noises.

She had her gun out, and Leblanc had his.

They moved into the woods, making their way carefully down the hill. She edged along, keeping low, staying under cover.

There. She could see a glimpse of the cabin ahead, nestled in the hillside. Trees flanked it, and there was a backdrop of rocky crags. A light gleamed dully in the window.

Leblanc's face was grim as he stared ahead.

"He's there," he whispered.

Beside the cabin was a shed, with a door. There were a few gaps in the wooden slats, and through them Katie thought she could see the dark shape of a vehicle. She wondered if this was the stolen car. It was invisible from the main road, but just visible to them in this stealthy approach. Without a doubt, Wolfe was here.

Given his track record so far, Katie was utterly sure that this stolen car was set as a trap. They needed to give it a wide berth and not under any circumstances open its doors.

But there would be other traps, too.

Hopefully, they were all set by a man who expected them to attack from the front. Even so, Katie knew they would need to be very careful.

Cautiously, they set off, pacing tentatively up the rocky track in the direction of the house.

She moved step by careful step, easing her way over the ground. And then, she jumped as Leblanc grabbed her wrist.

Katie's heart accelerated.

Ahead of them, as thin as a spider web, was a wire, stretched across the track at ankle height.

In the dark they would never have seen it. Now, in the early dawn, it was barely visible. It was amazing Leblanc had noticed it.

"We'd better step over," he breathed. "No other way around on this narrow path."

Katie felt dread surging inside her. She didn't like that he'd trapped this route. He should not even have guessed that they would take it. This showed how dangerous he was. He had prepared for every eventuality, and had not done what she'd predicted he would do.

Leblanc stepped carefully over the wire.

Katie held her breath, praying that he would be safe.

His feet scrunched on the ground. It held.

She followed him, stepping cautiously over, not wanting to think what could happen if this trap was triggered, or what might be waiting.

Only once she'd felt solid ground under her feet for a few steps did she relax.

But then, ahead of her, Leblanc let out a gasp.

The ground literally vanished from under him. Katie leapt to grab him, horror exploding inside her as Leblanc slipped and slid into a crevasse that had been concealed from view.

Ahead, the track had opened into a gaping, jagged chasm. It was a sudden, unexpected drop, like a trapdoor in the earth.

She managed to grasp his hand even as he was falling, clamping her hands over his, struggling to stop him from tumbling all the way down.

He was dangling over the side of the crevasse, just one hand in her grip. His face was twisted with panic.

She hauled back on his hand. Leblanc grabbed the lip of the crevasse with his other hand, but the packed ice and snow gave him no grip, and his hand slid away. She heard his breathing, harsh, panicked, mirroring her own.

In despair, she realized his weight was too heavy. In the snow, he was starting to pull her toward the brink of the crevasse.

With her feet sliding helplessly on the rocks and snow, Katie glanced around, desperate to find something she could use to anchor herself.

There was a sapling a yard away, thin but strong. Strong enough to take her weight? She hoped so. But it was too far away, and Leblanc's fingers were slipping. It would not be much longer before she couldn't hold him.

She had to try!

With a huge effort, Katie lunged for it, stretching her right arm out. She wrapped her hand around its trunk, grabbing it with all her strength.

She had it! And she still had hold of Leblanc. Now she could pull him to safety.

And then, the unthinkable happened.

The sapling flexed and snapped like a bow.

It had broken, and the impact had jerked Leblanc's hand out of hers.

With a terrible scraping, sliding noise, he vanished over the side of the crevasse.

She threw herself toward the edge, reaching out, desperate to catch hold of him, but the drop was too far, and he'd fallen into the shadows.

For an endless moment, there was only silence.

"Leblanc," she whispered. Her heart was banging in her throat. She couldn't take in the scale of this disaster.

There was no answer. He was gone.

Feeling sick with despair, she crawled to the brink of the crevasse and peered down.

She could not move, could not think. She was frozen. Her mind went blank, and she was numb.

Staring into the darkness, she saw it opened up into a long, steep slope. But it was not a sheer drop. He might just have survived the fall, but she couldn't see or hear anything. She listened, desperately trying to pick up sounds over the rush of the wind and her own panicked gasps.

Katie wanted to scream to him, to yell his name. But if Wolfe was nearby, that would alert him, and then they would both be in even worse danger.

"Leblanc," she whispered, but the wind smothered the sound and she heard no reply.

She could not shout louder. It was far too risky.

She listened again.

From far below, she thought she heard a soft, scraping sound. And then, a soft, regular tapping noise.

It might have been only her imagination, but she was sure she'd heard it.

Perhaps Leblanc was signaling her that he was alive and unhurt, trying to clamber to safety.

Or else, he was injured and desperately struggling to manage a serious bone break.

Her stomach twisted as she considered the possibilities, leaning over the brink of this chasm.

Chief among them was that Wolfe was listening for one or both of them to shout or scream. That would clue him that the trap had been triggered. That might be why there was no sound from below, where Leblanc would be thinking the same.

Her only hope was to keep quiet, and to try and find a way around to the bottom of the crevasse.

Leblanc might still be alive. She had to reach him before Wolfe did, or Katie knew it would be game over for both of them.

CHAPTER THIRTY ONE

Katie looked around her, drawing on the strength and resilience she'd developed during her training, and her dangerous career. Calmness was her friend now.

She fought for control, forcing herself to think clearly and logically, and to assess the terrain as she tried to devise the best way of getting down the steep, snowy slope. All her desperate worry about Leblanc, the emotions that surged inside her at the thought of him being badly hurt, or even losing him – all those had to be locked away.

Breathing out, Katie hoped she'd achieved the balance she needed.

Now, she had to find a safer way, some kind of route that would take her down to the base of the crevasse. There must be a way.

It was still barely light, and this western side of the slope was in semi-darkness.

She could see the crevasse clearly, but the surrounding ground was almost invisible in the thick banks of broken snow. It looked steep and slippery. The snow was glazed with ice. There was little chance of finding a safe or easy way down.

Katie grabbed onto a low tree branch, wondering if she could use it in place of a rope, to lower herself down. But she quickly realized it wouldn't work. The slope was too steep, and the branch didn't reach far enough.

She had to find a better way.

Moving around, she assessed her predicament while trying to see what she could use for purchase.

On the side of the path, she saw a rock shelf about six feet below her. It was just a few inches wide, but it looked like it might be solid. If she could reach it, she might be able to use it as a halfway point and descend the steep mountainside that way.

It was not a long drop beneath her, but it was narrow and unknown and intensely intimidating.

Could she do it?

Her heart beat fast with nerves and fear, but she had to try.

Katie leaned out, and let herself fall.

With a thud and a skid, she landed hard on the small rock ledge. It was just wide enough for her to stand on. Stones skidded and scattered, and shards of ice ricocheted away.

She scrambled quickly to keep her balance, but the surface was too icy. Her boots slid out from under her, and for a moment, she thought she was going to plummet into thin air.

Then, with a gasp, she found her footing. Now for the next step.

The tree nearby. If she could grab that, she could move to the lower side of the rock shelf. It was more solid there, and she could see what looked like a path beyond, curving steeply down, lined with small saplings that were tenaciously clinging to the unforgiving slope.

She seized hold of the tree, grabbed it with all her strength. Then she leaped forward, aiming for the more solid side of the rock shelf.

She flew through the air, aware of the dizzying drop beneath her.

And then she landed safely, her boots skidding on the rock.

She scrambled away from the edge. Her heart was pounding with terror and excitement. She'd made it! She had almost fallen to her death, but she was safe.

Now all she had to do was pick her way through the snow and brush that covered this track. Determinedly, she resolved to find Leblanc and help him to safety. Having gotten this far, she was sure she could succeed.

It was getting light all around her now, and she could see for miles, over the snowy hills and forests below, to the distant peaks of the mountains.

The path below was a steep, twisting route. It looked tricky. But she had no choice.

At least the trees on the side would provide her with some stability and a handhold.

She pushed her fear aside and stepped down, off the rocky ledge, her feet brushing through the sparse undergrowth that clung to the slope.

But as she took the next step, she felt, rather than saw, the wire loop tighten around her ankle.

It tautened suddenly, jerking her off her feet.

Screaming inwardly, with fear exploding inside her, Katie realized she'd triggered another trap. The trap that he'd set for exactly this purpose.

The sapling that had been forced into a tight loop was freed, and it wrenched her into the air, her stomach plummeting at the lack of control.

She sensed, rather than saw, that she was about to slam into a tree trunk, and covered her head with her arms.

Her wrist smashed into the trunk and she felt pain lance down her arm. Then her head bashed the tree, and stars erupted in her vision.

When they cleared, all she could see was the circle of the sky, and the branches and the leaves streaming by. She felt impossibly dizzy, and tensed, gasping for breath, as she waited for the inevitable impact with the ground.

But she didn't crash into the ground.

She stayed dangling in the air, upside down, the noose around her ankle pulling her tight. She could feel the constricting pressure of it, cutting into her flesh. She tasted blood in her mouth. She looked down and saw the ground far, far below her.

Flailing her arms and legs, her head whirling, Katie tried to grab on to something, anything.

She could barely breathe as she struggled against the bite of the wire, blood streaming from her arm. She felt giddy, disoriented. Gasping for air. Her head started to pound.

With all her might, she struggled against the wire, trying to pull on it, to slip her foot out of the noose. She needed to get some slack on it so she could maneuver, before it got tighter still.

She had to do something to loosen this wire.

But she was swiftly realizing it was a bad idea. The blood was rushing to her head and her struggles were worsening the dizziness. Her head was spinning, her vision blurred.

With a sense of doom, she knew she was starting to lose consciousness. The lack of air combined with her struggles was taking its toll.

Blackness started to bubble up around her, covering her, dimming her vision, curbing her struggles.

Just before the shadows swallowed her, Katie thought she saw a tall man approach, making his way inexorably toward her.

It was too late. She was trapped.

Wolfe had won.

CHAPTER THIRTY TWO

Katie's head was pounding as daylight and consciousness slowly filtered back.

She was alive.

She couldn't believe that. In fact, she was utterly shocked to be breathing again, and to be able to open her eyes, feeling cold and pain – but at least, feeling.

Was she okay?

She was lying on a hard and bitterly cold floor. Staring up at a dark ceiling. From somewhere nearby, muted light was filtering in. Her vision was still blurry and her head was spinning.

She couldn't move her arms or legs and felt a surge of panic. Was she paralyzed?

Then, as her mind caught up, she realized she was firmly restrained. Her arms were tied behind her. Rope bit into her wrists.

Her legs were bound, too. She could move them, slowly, but they felt numb. She blinked, and her vision slowly cleared.

Craning her neck, Katie looked around, and found that she could just about make out the shape of a workbench in front of her, and a tall, narrow window nearby. It was flanked by wooden walls and she realized, with a shock, that she must be in Wolfe's cabin. He'd brought her here and he had left her, trussed.

Where had he gone?

Her thoughts spun immediately to Leblanc. She'd tried to save him. Did Wolfe know where he was? Had he seem him?

Was Leblanc even still alive?

First things first, Katie told herself, glad that at this frantic moment, the discipline of her training allowed her to think clearly and not succumb to the desperation simmering inside her.

First thing, you try to get out of these ties.

She found that she was able to push herself into a sitting position.

Her head was swimming. She was still wearing her coat, but her boots, her gloves and her scarf were gone. No wonder she was freezing cold, and her hands and feet felt numb. He'd taken her gun. Her holster was empty.

How could she free herself?

Her hands felt firmly tied.

The rough rope knotting her ankles together was also tight. Katie couldn't figure out any way to get to something that might cut it. Perhaps the easiest way would be to unpick the knots.

Katie jackknifed onto her side and stretched her legs up behind her, reaching her heels to the small of her back. She breathed deeply as her quads threatened to cramp.

But she could touch the knots in her ankle ties with her trussed fingers. Just.

Patiently, with her muscles screaming at the tightness of her hand ties, Katie worked on the knots. She worked on the edges of the rough strands, feeling in place of seeing. But nothing helped. She was not able to undo these knots.

Perhaps there was some kind of tool she could use, if she was able to struggle to her feet?

But, as she scrambled to her knees, she heard footfalls approaching from outside.

Panic surged inside her. Was Wolfe coming back?

The door creaked and Katie's stomach lurched as she braced herself for another confrontation, and a probable kill, because there was no way she could defend herself.

The door swung slowly open.

To her astonishment, she found herself staring at Leblanc.

He was limping, breathing hard. There was blood on his face and on his coat. His clothing was scratched and torn. His gun holster was gone. The fall must have ripped it off his waist.

But he was alive. Relief made her dizzy all over again. Somehow, he had managed to scramble out from the ravine and had survived the fall without any major injuries.

He looked just as astounded to see her.

"Katie," he whispered. "Are you okay?"

"I am. But I need my wrists untied." She staggered up. Her feet were numb and freezing. "Where is he?" she asked, with dread now darkening her joy.

If he'd been looking for Leblanc and hadn't found him, he would be here very soon.

"I don't know," he said. "I haven't seen him."

Leblanc moved quickly over to her and began wrestling with the ties around her feet. She felt his fingers struggling with the knots. They were tight, and his hands were also freezing. Katie sensed they didn't have any time left, that Wolfe was going to come back any moment, and that they would then be in a deadly confrontation.

On the table, she saw a cartridge case for a shotgun. He must be out with his gun, and she felt sure he was ready to use it now.

Up until now, he had not used a gun. For whatever reason had prevailed in his paranoid and unstable mind, he had started out trapping them. But she guessed the time for that was over now, and that his thoughts would be first to trap, and then to kill.

It would not be long before he followed Leblanc's tracks up to the cabin.

"There. I've got your feet done. Now for your hands," he said.

The tight ropes fell away and Katie flexed her ankles, which felt stiff and sore. Her feet were tingling as the blood rushed back.

"I need to get this done fast," Leblanc said, gritting his teeth as he tugged at the knots. He glanced at the wall.

"There's something that will help." He sounded relieved.

Looking around, Katie saw he was right. An old saw hung on a hook on the wall.

She felt ashamed she hadn't noticed it. She should have spotted it earlier, but she'd been too dizzy and had not been observant enough of her surroundings.

By now, she could have freed herself if she'd been sharper! Katie felt self-blame fill her. That saw was at head height. She could have grabbed the handle in her teeth, sawed through her ankle ropes, and then trapped the handle between her legs and cut through her wrist ties. Instead, Leblanc had wasted precious minutes struggling with the knots which were only now starting to loosen.

But, as Leblanc stepped forward to lift the saw off the wall, the floorboard he was standing on collapsed.

With a cry, he tumbled downward. Then he gave another, surprised yell.

"Leblanc. What's happened?" Katie said, anxiety flaring as she rushed forward.

"Keep back! There are spikes here. Barbed spikes. My boots are totally stuck. I think one of them has pierced my foot."

With a flood of horror, Katie realized that was why Wolfe had removed her shoes. He'd intended for her to see the saw, and try to reach it. In her bare feet, she would have plunged down onto the spikes,

147

which would have pierced right through her soles, stabbing all the way through her feet, trapping and injuring her beyond help.

This had progressed beyond simple trapping. This was torture. He'd escalated his agenda, she realized with a shiver.

Leblanc was wearing heavy winter boots. Their solid soles had saved him but he was pinned. Katie thought he might have to struggle out of his footwear to get free.

Groaning, Leblanc pitched forward onto his hands, taking the weight off his feet before the brutal spikes could pierce right through his soles and cause him serious hurt.

"Stay away," he warned her. "Don't come and help. Who knows what else is going to be set off here?"

"Okay," she murmured back, wishing she could help but acknowledging it was too dangerous. Instead, gritting her teeth, Katie fought against the ropes, hoping that Leblanc had worked them loose enough for her to yank her hands free.

At last, she felt the knots start to give.

And then, she glanced through the cabin window and saw her worst nightmare.

Wolfe was pacing up the hill, a small, faraway figure, holding his shotgun and heading purposefully in the direction of the cabin.

Katie drew in a deep breath, her mind racing. This was too soon. There was no time for them to get away, or regroup, or even muster any defense beyond the rusty saw.

He had them where he wanted them and she had no doubt, now, that he was moving in for the kill. Neither of them had a firearm. Katie had no shoes and no idea where they were. And her arms were still trussed behind her, although she'd unpicked one side of the knot. Leblanc was trapped in spikes and trying to free himself.

"He's coming," she said.

"I'll be out in a minute!" Leblanc gasped. "You go! Run! You can get away in time. Get back to where we left the car."

"I don't think so," she snarled. That was out of the question. No way was she going to abandon her partner.

Now was the time to stand and fight - but how? She had only a couple of minutes to try to act before Wolfe reached the cabin.

With a mighty tug, she finally managed to free her wrists.

"I'm out!" Leblanc gasped at the same time. He'd left his shoes behind, entangled in the blades.

She was barefoot and her gun was gone, but at least she had the use of her hands.

Suddenly, Katie realized what they could do. They did, in fact, have a weapon to use.

She only had the shortest time to prepare, but hoped that her reckless, last-minute plan would turn the tables on their adversary.

*

Two breathless minutes later, she heard Wolfe's footsteps, heavy and purposeful as he trudged through the snow and up to the door.

Katie waited behind the door. This entire cobbled-together scenario was risky, but this was one of the most dangerous parts.

"Where's the man?" she heard him mutter as he approached. "He must be here? She must have brought him here!"

He sounded paranoid, aggressive, but there was an edge of triumph in his tone.

As he strode inside, she burst out to meet him, as fast as she could, needing not just the element of surprise, but the force of total shock.

She saw him briefly for the first time ever. White face, dark, furious eyes, short-cropped, untidy hair. His shoulders were big in his fur coat. His gun was slung over his shoulder; he hadn't expected to need it.

Immediately, she shoved him in the chest hard, so that he staggered backward. Slipping back onto the snow, he let out a roar of rage.

Katie fled, heading for the lean-to where the car was parked. She flung open the wooden door and burst in.

"Where is he?" Wolfe roared. "The man! Where is he?" His feet pounded behind her.

"He's in here! Don't hurt me! He's in here!"

She rushed into the lean-to, cowering away behind the stolen Land Rover. Breathing heavily, he pursued her. With anger and fear emanating from him, he stormed toward her. Now he was taking his gun off his shoulder, but he couldn't easily use it in this confined space. He expected to find Leblanc hiding here, but he would be disappointed.

As he powered toward her, Katie sprinted around the other side of the car and veered back to the shack door, racing as fast as she could to get out.

For just a moment, Wolfe hesitated, surprised by the fact his quarry was not where she'd said he would be.

Then he turned and rushed to catch her.

But she had already reached the shack's doorway. As she burst out, Leblanc was waiting, his hands on the door. Throwing all his weight against it, he shoved it closed. He only just got it fastened in time, as Wolfe began battering on it.

Katie's breath burned in her lungs as she picked up the end of the wire she'd attached to the car door.

Wolfe was yelling in anger, ripping at the flimsy boards. Then, with a deafening crack, a gunshot split the air and a hole appeared in the rotted wood.

Adrenaline surging, Katie ducked. Then, with all her strength, she pulled the wire.

Inside the lean-to, the car door flew open.

There was a pause. Just long enough for her to doubt herself, terrified that her plan had not worked and she'd read his mind wrong.

Then, she heard a sizzle, followed by the sharp crackle of flames, and a howl of fear from Wolfe inside.

His trap had been triggered, but he was the one who would not escape it.

Flames erupted as smoke filled the shed.

Leblanc grabbed Katie's hand and they ran for it, hot-footing it around the side of the building. Katie's feet stung in the snow.

A moment later, an explosion split the air, shaking the cabin walls, resounding around the valley, echoing in the emptiness.

Katie sagged to a stop, her breath burning in her lungs. She couldn't quite believe that they'd done it. She felt deeply relieved, but at the same time she couldn't help feeling a sense of regret that this paranoid, deluded man had clearly been beyond any help or redemption. His damaged mind had caused him to become the victim of his own trap.

CHAPTER THIRTY THREE

Katie jerked awake, briefly disoriented. She'd fallen asleep in the helicopter on the way home, exhausted to the bone after this case that had literally taken them all the way to the wire.

Embarrassed, she realized she'd been leaning against Leblanc, cuddled into his shoulder. Her dreams had been calm. Comforting.

Had his arm been around her? That was a strange thought. She had the feeling that as she'd woken, some sort of hasty rearrangement had occurred.

But it could have been the pilot, banking the helicopter sharply as he came in to land.

They were arriving back in her home town - home for now, anyway - the border city of Sault Ste Marie. It seemed a world away from this morning's battleground.

After the explosion, Wolfe's shack had burned to the ground.

An hour later, helicopters had landed, and the local police had arrived to record the scene and remove the body. They'd proceeded with extreme caution. Eight more traps had been identified and carefully dismantled.

Katie had helped them construct a narrative of her progress and Wolfe's movements. A medic had then landed to check them out, and had treated their fortunately minor injuries.

Now, they were home, and as they touched down, her phone started ringing. It was Scott on the line.

This time, she could feel real relief as she answered, switching the phone to speaker so Leblanc could also hear.

"Katie. Congratulations to you and Leblanc. That was an extremely tough case. I'm glad you cracked it. I never doubted you would," he said.

The praise made her feel warm inside.

"It was a tough one. It could so easily have gone wrong," she agreed. "But we managed."

The noisy blades had gone quiet. The helicopter door opened, and cool, fresh afternoon air filtered in.

151

"We've released Marius Roman. He's going back home. I don't imagine he'll cause any trouble."

"Thank you," Katie said, glad that the deal she'd made with Wolfe's father had been honored.

"The fire brigade have finally gotten into the shack, and they have found Wolfe's body there. So it's case closed. We've notified Marius. He didn't seem sad. If anything, he sounded relieved," Scott said thoughtfully.

That chilled Katie. Who knew how far Wolfe's murderous agenda would have taken him?

"Take the day off tomorrow. You two need a break. If there's anything urgent, the others can handle it."

"Thanks," Katie said gratefully. She could use a day's rest, that was for sure.

She disconnected the call, and they climbed out of the chopper.

"Can I give you a ride home?" Leblanc asked.

"Thanks," Katie said.

They walked companionably to the parking lot where Leblanc's unmarked waited, and climbed inside. He headed out, on the short drive downtown to where her apartment was.

"What are you going to do tomorrow?" he asked.

Katie hesitated. Was this a leading question? She wasn't sure.

"I'm seeing my mentor, Timms, for brunch. He's now working as a criminal law consultant. He's meeting up with a colleague in Sudbury, and is making a stop to see me first. It'll be great to catch up with him."

She smiled, thinking of the support that this knowledgeable agent had given her in her early career. She knew Timms would be fascinated to hear about her last few cases, particularly this recent one.

Deciding to keep Leblanc's question open-ended, she countered with her own.

"What about you?" she asked.

Now, to her surprise, Leblanc looked slightly uneasy.

"A friend of mine just messaged. An ex-colleague from Paris. She's en-route to Vancouver, and making a stopover. I'm seeing her for lunch tomorrow."

Katie raised internal eyebrows, remembering that strange phone call Leblanc had taken while in the woods.

She wasn't sure this colleague was just a colleague. She sensed that Leblanc was embroiled in an internal struggle, and wondered if there were factors in play she didn't yet know about.

Both of their schedules left the evening open, but Katie wasn't going to be the one to suggest anything. Perhaps it was better to not, she thought. Perhaps they should both steer away from the mutual attraction that was growing between them.

It would be safer, for sure.

But then again, safety wasn't why she'd taken on this job.

With a flicker of excitement, Katie remembered that the case notes from her sister's murder file were due to be sent to her. Leblanc had done what she'd asked, and the case had been reopened. If those arrived in time, she could spend tomorrow night revising them, and see if anything untoward grabbed her interest.

She was sure there would be inconsistencies to be found.

Alternatively, she might just get a last-minute dinner invite.

Who knew?

Leblanc pulled up outside her apartment.

"Thanks for the ride," she said.

"No problem," he replied.

They both waited a beat. Then, smiling to herself, Katie nodded.

"See you soon," she said.

She turned and walked inside, wondering what surprises tomorrow would bring.

EPILOGUE

Leblanc waited at the airport. It felt strange to be back here less than twenty-four hours after he'd landed, and even stranger to be meeting the woman he'd seen in Paris only a few days earlier.

His heart sped up as he saw Eloise stride into the arrivals hall.

Petite, dynamic, and with a strong, beautiful face that lit up when she saw him.

But he couldn't feel the excitement that he knew he should.

There were so many complications. This developing situation meant there was a decision to be made, and it was not a small one, but rather something that could change his life.

Did it need changing? That was the question.

But there was no time to think about answers as she hugged him hard.

"Lovely to see you! I am excited to be here. Where shall we go for lunch? Can we do a tour through the town? I need to see it!"

"What time is your flight this evening?" he asked.

"It's at seven. So we have a few hours to spare."

Her arm linked through his and they walked out of the airport.

"What a beautiful city," she enthused, as they headed to the parking. "As I flew in, I looked down. It is so scenic, so unusual."

"I've been surprised by how I've enjoyed it here," Leblanc agreed, opening the car door for her.

"I can see why you want to stay," she said, as he got in. "But that makes my visit even more problematic."

"Why's that?" he asked, feeling suddenly nervous.

"Because I have an actual offer for you. Should you choose to accept it, of course," she said.

"An offer?" He could hear the incredulity in his own voice.

"Yes. A senior detective is retiring in May. He heads up the central Paris precinct. This is a very prestigious position. More seniority, higher pay grade, and also more of a management job and less of a feet-on-the-ground. Perhaps, at thirty-five, that would suit you?"

Her glance flickered his way.

"You're telling me this, why?" he asked, wanting to confirm exactly what the situation was.

"Because I put your name forward as his successor. And based on your past record and current experience, they are very interested to speak to you."

"Eloise, I - I can't believe it!"

Leblanc felt as if he'd been punched in the stomach - but not in a bad way, this time. Just in a shocking way. He literally could not believe this offer. It felt as if the rug had been ripped from under him. Everything had shifted.

His decisions so far felt fragile, questionable. The sense of confidence he'd felt yesterday had dissolved.

"You don't have to decide immediately. If you want to take the job, you need to let them know in two weeks. Otherwise, they will advertise it publicly," she explained.

"I - I see. Thank you."

He didn't know what else to say or how to handle this.

"That's why I came here. To tell you in person. We can discuss more over lunch. But there's something else, also."

Now her voice dropped, and he leaned in closer.

She sounded as serious as she ever had.

"It's to do with Gagnon. You know him, of course? Cecile's killer."

Leblanc's head swam. Was she reading his mind? Had she somehow intuited the terrible thoughts he'd been having about this man, his dreams of revenge?

"What about him?" he asked, his mouth dry, wanting to know, yet not wanting.

"It's serious," she said, her voice hard. "I can't say more now. It's confidential, and I'm not allowed to. If you come back to Paris, and take the job, you'll find out what it is, and be able to make a decision accordingly. If not, then you should leave it be."

She stared at him, and he saw clearly the unspoken bargain she had laid out.

Which would it be?

Find out more, get closer, take the job and become involved in whatever this situation was with Gagnon - and although his mind was racing, he had no clear idea what it could be.

Or walk away forever.

The choice was clear. It was hard, and the implications would be lasting.

Leblanc had no idea what he should choose. His head was telling him one thing, his heart another. He needed more time. He knew he had two weeks to make a final decision about applying for the job, but right now, he owed her an answer.

He took a deep breath, hoping for the courage to voice what he thought was right.

NOW AVAILABLE!

HELP ME
(A Katie Winter FBI Suspense Thriller —Book 5)

A new serial killer strikes outside of Seattle, and FBI Special Agent Katie Winter is summoned when he crosses the border to strike in Vancouver, too. With victims tied to logs and sent downriver, it appears this is the work of a deranged logger—and yet, after a shocking twist, Katie, facing her own demons, realizes that nothing is what it seems.

"Molly Black has written a taut thriller that will keep you on the edge of your seat… I absolutely loved this book and can't wait to read the next book in the series!"
—Reader review for Girl One: Murder

HELP ME is book #5 in a new series by #1 bestselling mystery and suspense author Molly Black.

FBI Special Agent Katie Winter is no stranger to frigid winters, isolation, and dangerous cases. With her sterling record of hunting down serial killers, she is a fast-rising star in the BAU, and Katie is the natural choice to partner with Canadian law enforcement to track killers across brutal and unforgiving landscapes.

Will Katie enter the killer's mind in time to save the next victim?

A complex psychological crime thriller full of twists and turns and packed with heart-pounding suspense, the KATIE WINTER mystery series will make you fall in love with a brilliant new female protagonist and keep you turning pages late into the night.

Book #6 in the series—FORGET ME—is now also available.

"I binge read this book. It hooked me in and didn't stop till the last few pages… I look forward to reading more!"
—Reader review for Found You

"I loved this book! Fast-paced plot, great characters and interesting insights into investigating cold cases. I can't wait to read the next book!"
—Reader review for Girl One: Murder

"Very good book… You will feel like you are right there looking for the kidnapper! I know I will be reading more in this series!"
—Reader review for Girl One: Murder

"This is a very well written book and holds your interest from page 1… Definitely looking forward to reading the next one in the series, and hopefully others as well!"
—Reader review for Girl One: Murder

"Wow, I cannot wait for the next in this series. Starts with a bang and just keeps going."
—Reader review for Girl One: Murder

"Well written book with a great plot, one that will keep you up at night. A page turner!"
—Reader review for Girl One: Murder

"A great suspense that keeps you reading… can't wait for the next in this series!"
—Reader review for Found You

"Sooo soo good! There are a few unforeseen twists… I binge read this like I binge watch Netflix. It just sucks you in."
—Reader review for Found You

Molly Black

Bestselling author Molly Black is author of the MAYA GRAY FBI suspense thriller series, comprising nine books (and counting); of the RYLIE WOLF FBI suspense thriller series, comprising six books (and counting); of the TAYLOR SAGE FBI suspense thriller series, comprising three books (and counting); and of the KATIE WINTER FBI suspense thriller series, comprising six books (and counting).

An avid reader and lifelong fan of the mystery and thriller genres, Molly loves to hear from you, so please feel free to visit www.mollyblackauthor.com to learn more and stay in touch.

BOOKS BY MOLLY BLACK

MAYA GRAY MYSTERY SERIES
GIRL ONE: MURDER (Book #1)
GIRL TWO: TAKEN (Book #2)
GIRL THREE: TRAPPED (Book #3)
GIRL FOUR: LURED (Book #4)
GIRL FIVE: BOUND (Book #5)
GIRL SIX: FORSAKEN (Book #6)
GIRL SEVEN: CRAVED (Book #7)
GIRL EIGHT: HUNTED (Book #8)
GIRL NINE: GONE (Book #9)

RYLIE WOLF FBI SUSPENSE THRILLER
FOUND YOU (Book #1)
CAUGHT YOU (Book #2)
SEE YOU (Book #3)
WANT YOU (Book #4)
TAKE YOU (Book #5)
DARE YOU (Book #6)

TAYLOR SAGE FBI SUSPENSE THRILLER
DON'T LOOK (Book #1)
DON'T BREATHE (Book #2)
DON'T RUN (Book #3)

KATIE WINTER FBI SUSPENSE THRILLER
SAVE ME (Book #1)
REACH ME (Book #2)
HIDE ME (Book #3)
BELIEVE ME (Book #4)
HELP ME (Book #5)
FORGET ME (Book #6)

Lightning Source UK Ltd.
Milton Keynes UK
UKHW040232210223
417160UK00022B/110